I0771609

It's Rough Out There

By Michol Whitney

It's Rough Out There

Copyright © 2024

Paperback ISBN: **979-8-9877569-4-2**

Written by Michol Whitney
Illustrations by Kayla Hartgrove

Enjoy the adventure!

www.write2readright.com
Email: smithwhitney@write2readright.com

For Chad, Ohmari, Rayven, Will, Madison, Jayden,

Aminah, Austin, Autumn, and Aubrii

and to all my students at CPS and Zoe Life

It's Rough Out There

By Michol Whitney

Chapter 1

Comfort in the Rough

It amazes me how many people like living in this rough neighborhood. There are many vacant buildings and empty lots. Graffiti covers some buildings, litter is almost everywhere, a lot of people are noisy, and there is a great deal of crime. My dad said this is because income and economic inequality has taken a drastic toll on this neighborhood over the years. Still, my parents will not move us somewhere nicer.

My name is Jamal, and I am ten years old. I get my name from my dad's middle name. His first name is James, but people around here call him Jamal. They call me Junior, and I answer out of respect, but I am not a junior. Jamal means handsome, so naturally, I prefer to be called Jamal. My mom's name is Azania, and my dad calls her Azza. Her parents are from Durban, South Africa, and they chose her name because it was used mainly as a symbol of resistance during the apartheid era in South Africa, and boy, does she make it a point to live up to her name.

As I mentioned, we live in a rough neighborhood where things get crazy sometimes, but my mom and dad love it here. My mom refuses to leave this neighborhood. She always says she would rather live here than in a community where she is not welcomed, wanted, or respected. My dad shares the same feeling, so I cannot convince them to leave, but that does not stop me from trying.

My dad's side of the family lives in a nearby neighborhood. He has vowed to stay close to his family and friends because he believes families should live close enough to help and be there for one another. He has a big family of three brothers, five sisters, aunts, uncles, and countless cousins. He is always there for them when they need him, and they are here for him when he needs them.

Our neighborhood is huge, and my dad is familiar with every block, store, car wash, and park. You name it, and he can tell you all about it. His favorite spot in our neighborhood is the pond. He loves fishing because it challenges him, brings him in touch with the outdoors to escape the noisy city life, and gives us time to bond. He does not consider fishing a sport; instead, he calls it a skill and sets personal goals on each fishing trip. He enjoys reeling in the big fish and bragging about his catches.

I'm not a fan of fishing, but I love spending time with my dad. He works many hard hours during the week and sometimes on weekends, so we get up early and head to the pond whenever he has a weekend off. In addition, my dad is an excellent cook, so a successful Saturday morning fishing trip makes for an even better Saturday evening fish fry.

I always look forward to a good fish fry even though I do not like having to catch the fish. I would much rather spend my Saturday mornings in bed. Especially after the night I had. Last night was like any other Friday night in the summer, and a lot was happening in the neighborhood. It was hot, and our area was boisterous. Summer had barely started, but the sun was already heating the air. The day was so hot that not many people were out, but when it slowly cooled down at night, people took advantage of the drop in temperature and headed to the streets.

Our house is close to a busy street and only steps away from the quiet pond. There is a park near the pond with a playground for kids. Unfortunately, on weekends the park becomes a playground for

older teens and young adults that hang out there.
They blast their music, and play loudly, making it
hard for people like me to sleep at night. Starting on
Juneteenth, they treat every weekend like the Fourth
of July and shoot off noisy fireworks. Then, of
course, I must mention all the sirens I hear. Police
cars, fire trucks, and ambulances have distinct wails
and howls that play through the night.

I tried to force myself to sleep last night
because I knew my dad would be off work today,
and we would get up early and go fishing.
Unfortunately, I am not a morning person, so I am
never in the mood for early wake-up calls, but it is
inevitable. My dad cheerfully knocked on my door
and came inside. He shook my bed and pulled the
covers from over my head. Little did he know, I had
barely just gone to sleep.

"Yo! It's time to get up!" Dad said as he stood over
my bed.

It took all I had to pretend to be excited
about our fishing trip. My covers did not want to let

me go, nor did I want to part with them. I was annoyed with my dad and his upbeat, over-the-top, cheerful demeanor, but I could not let him know. I wondered how he could sleep well through the night with all that was happening in the neighborhood last night.

Our house is small, and my bedroom is tiny and cluttered. It is a somewhat manageable room, but I have to keep my sport equipment and bicycle in my room because we do not have enough storage space. My twin-sized bed and desk take up the most space making it hard for me to get around. You would think the lack of space in our home would be an incentive to move, but my parents are content with the space we have.

"Good morning, Dad," I said as I stretched and tried to force a smile, but it was not happening.

"It sure is, so let's get out and make the most of it," he said. Before I knew it, he trampled through the clutter to get to my window and open the curtains, and then he briskly walked out of my room.

I forced myself out of bed and headed down the hall to the bathroom. I could smell bacon and eggs from the kitchen, which motivated me to put more pep in my step. I peeked into my parent's bedroom to speak to my mom, and she stopped making the bed to blow me a kiss. They have a small bedroom too. However, their room is not cluttered because my dad drilled shelves into their walls to store things.

"Good morning, Jamal," she said as she went back to making the bed.

On Saturdays, when we go fishing, dad cooks breakfast while my mom enjoys a few minutes more of sleep. Fishing days are usually pretty chill, but family and friends are coming over today. Although hot, the weather was in our favor, so my parents decided to have a fish fry to celebrate the start of summer. Our family celebrates everything, and we usually celebrate with lots of food. My parents both come by this honestly because of family traditions. My dad considers himself the bar-b-que king, and my mom considers herself the braai (brī) queen. Braai is the South African version of barbeque, which means grilled meat. No matter what you call it, they both take grilling very seriously.

Like Americans, South Africans have many occasions to celebrate, which usually means lots of good food is involved. In September, when South Africans celebrate Heritage Day, my mom celebrates here by whipping up her favorite meals from back home in Africa. She grills her favorite South African dishes, and we celebrate in honor of her customs as a family. On Heritage Day, she makes Bunny Chow. She grills meat to make a stew and then stuffs the stew into a gutted-out loaf of bread. It is delicious, but Heritage Day is usually the only day she makes it.

My mom's family moved to the United States when my mother was young. When she married my dad, her parents had already moved back to Durban. We are going to visit my grandparents in Durban soon. I have never been to South Africa, but I hear they have fantastic beaches.

I often try to convince my mother that we should move there just to get away from here. Anywhere must be better than where we live now.

After getting dressed, I went to the kitchen to have breakfast. My dad had a plate set up for my mom and me. He finished his coffee and placed our fishing gear near the front door. Just once, I would like to see the fishing gear near the back door. At least then, I would know we would be driving to the pond. Unfortunately, my dad never uses the car to get to places close enough to walk.

"It will be a hot one," dad insisted, "you better grab a hat and your sunglasses."

After eating, I grabbed my things and followed my dad. While walking to the pond, my dad asked me random questions about sports and cars. We both love American muscle cars, and he has trained my ears to know the sounds of their engines. It is too early to hear those engines now, but we may see or hear a muscle car or two on the way home. We talked a little about my grades and school, but then he went for the jugular and asked about the girls in my class. Of course, I'm not interested in any of them, but he insists that there has to be one girl that I find special. Of course, he is wrong, so that discussion is always brief, and I cleverly change the subject to talking about fishing.

"Looks like our spot is open," he says. "We can get set up over here," he continued to place the tackle box down to take a collapsible chair out of the bag. I found a spot close to him and set up my chair. My dad has a routine for setting up our area, and I know it well. He is always aware of his surroundings, so first, he scans the area carefully before and after picking a spot to set up. Then, after setting up the chairs, he gets his phone out and starts his fishing playlist. He has a playlist for everything. He has a playlist for cooking, cleaning, washing his car, and changing the oil. All his playlists have different songs. His lists go from old school to new school, R&B to gospel, and he knows the lyrics to every song on his lists. You can bet he will hum each melody if the song is instrumental.

Now that the chairs are in place and his playlist is on, he turns the music down so low that we can barely hear it. He never plays the music loud, so we don't have to yell to talk to each other. He also believes loud music will scare off the fish. Most importantly, he wants to hear what is going on around us. He constantly scans the park. He watches our surroundings like a spy, and he watches the water as though he can see the fish through the water's surface.

"Dad," I pause and look at him as he gets the hooks and bait out of the tackle box. He looks at me, waiting for me to continue, but I can't. I am unsure if this is the best time to ask about moving to another neighborhood, and I regret even getting his attention. However, I cannot leave him hanging; now will have to be just as good a time as any.

"Last night was rough. The sirens and loud music kept me up late. I could barely sleep, and I was very uncomfortable. Can we please move to another quieter neighborhood?" I asked, unsure what to expect because I realized this was not the best time to discuss moving.

He calmly answered, "I grew up here, and so did your mother. We just happen to like this neighborhood. It has lots of good memories." My dad explained as he went back to gathering the materials for fishing. "If it was good enough for us, it's good enough for you," he demanded, and I mocked him by moving my lips in sync with his. "Besides, this is our home. You should want to be here."

"But I do not feel safe here," I said. "Living here makes me feel uncomfortable."

My dad did not respond; instead, he handed me a container of live worms. I have never told him how much I disliked using live bait for fishing, and I hoped my face did not show how disgusted I was by the squirming, fat worms. Don't get me wrong, I catch worms and chase my friends with them for fun. Worms aren't gross, but poking the hook through them to use for bait is. He watched as I threaded the worms through the hook. My dad has been fishing since he was very young. He is used to threading these little boogers, but I will never get used to poking, squeezing and pushing them through the hook. That is just disgusting.

Dad spent many days at this pond as a child with his dad, and when his dad could no longer take him fishing due to illness, he would go fishing with his best friend Xavier and Xavier's dad. Xavier's dad would fall asleep with his hat over his eyes, and my dad and Xavier would get into all kinds of mischief. He has told me at least one hundred stories of how much fun he and Xavier had at the pond. He showed me the trees they used to climb and use as a safety base when they played tag. My dad showed me the tree at the pond, where he nervously kissed my mom for the first time. Then, before she went away to college, he proposed to her at that same tree just a few years later. He enjoys telling me stories, and I love hearing them, but he never talks about how Xavier lost his life to gun violence.

Someone killed Xavier here, which should

be enough to justify why it is not safe to live here. Why would he act as though living here is okay when it is not? If he thinks this is such a nice place for us to live, he owes me an explanation of how he came to that conclusion. It is so rough here that you must be tough to survive. He and my mom must be the only people in the neighborhood who like living here. I don't understand it.

"Dad," I looked at my dad to see if he seemed annoyed. "Do you feel safe here?" I asked.

"Do I feel safe here?" he laughed as he repeated the question I had literally just asked him. Then, after a brief pause, he confidently answered, "Absolutely! I feel safe everywhere I go. Are you forgetting that I grew up here and that these are my stomping grounds?" he asked. "Stop being so afraid of everything. I feel safe here and everywhere else. The only things that should be afraid are all the fish we will catch." He walked close to the pond's edge and scanned the water again. "Now let's get 'em!" he said as he gestured, titling his head for me to get started.

Chapter 2

Troubling Times

I took my fishing pole to the water's edge but did
not cast my rod. I always watch my dad cast his rod
first. He is always very strategic. He has a routine
for casting his rod. First, he secures his feet, and
then he stretches his arms. Next, he moves his head
from side to side and quickly flicks his rod from
behind and toward the water. I always chuckle at
how intense he is, but I do the same thing.

Last year, I mimicked my dad's casting routine, but
I didn't have enough grip on the handle, and when I
casted my rod over my shoulder, I threw the whole
fishing rod into the water. I laughed out of
embarrassment, but my dad did not find it funny. As
serious as my dad is about fishing, I imagined he
would have made me go into the murky pond to get
the rod out. Of course, he knew I didn't mean to let
it go, but I tend to think the worst of things

sometimes. It turns out he did not get upset at all. He only told me, "Next time, secure your grip on the handle before you cast your rod." That was it. I had to practice casting away from the water a few times before using the spare rod, but I learned my lesson, and it has not happened again.

This year, I am older and only require a little assistance. It was my turn to cast my line in the water. I concentrated on where I wanted the hook to land, like a baseball player pointing to where he wanted his hit to land. My dad watched me from the corner of his eyes. He pretended to focus on where his hook landed. He bobbed his head to the music playing softly in the background, but I knew he was watching me; he always does. After getting a good grip on the handle of the fishing rod, I cast out my line. The red and white floater drifted in the air, landing on the spot next to my dad's. I was impressed, and so was my dad. He did not tell me he was impressed, but I saw him try to hide the smile on his face.

It was early, but I could feel the sun shining

in our direction. As I looked around, I could see a family of ducks entering the pond and geese flying over where we were. There were hardly any clouds, but the ones that were there were white and fluffy, and I enjoyed watching them move quickly as others passed by slowly in the gentle breeze. As I watched the clouds, a plane passed, and I imagined the passengers going somewhere tropical. I wished I was on that plane to get away from here; even though it was peaceful at the pond, I knew it would not be like this at nightfall.

We waited patiently as we watched the occasional breeze make a small, gentle ripple on the water's surface, but that was about the only movement we saw on the pond; that, and a few insects land on the plants growing in the pond. The sounds in our surroundings are random. We hear a car passing here and there and birds chirping in the distance, but all the while, my dad's music is playing softly. The songs on his playlist predate him by nearly twenty years, but he knows every word to every song, and I am learning them too. Even shuffling the playlist, he knows what song will come on next and is ready to hum along quietly.

"How about now?" he said out of nowhere.

"Huh?" I thoughtlessly answered. One of my dad's biggest pet peeves is hearing someone say, huh. He believes intelligent people should have and use a broader, more intelligent vocabulary. I tried to stop myself, but it slipped out faster than I could think of anything else to say. I knew he would be annoyed by my perfunctory response, so I quickly tried to fix it.

"I mean… not, huh. I meant to say, how about who? No! I mean, how about what?" Now I really sound silly.

"Relax," he said with a chuckle. "How about now?" he probed as he looked at me. "Do you feel safe right now?" He took his eyes off the water and looked at me. I did not want to hurt his feelings. He loves this neighborhood and the people here. It had been quiet for so long that I forgot I had asked him about moving to a different area.

"I only feel safe when you are with me, but

even then, I do not like living here," I answered, trying not to hurt his feelings but being honest about how I feel. "I like when you are around. You are brave and strong, but you can't always be around. When you are not around, I do not feel safe." I moaned as I relaxed my fishing rod. He raised his chin to signal to me to lift the rod. As I raised my rod, he looked back at the water.

"You shouldn't only feel safe when I am around," he insisted. "You are a part of me. What I have, you have too. So, if you think that I am brave and strong, you should feel brave and strong, too, because you get it from me." He said as he did a confident laugh and went back to adjusting his fishing pole. "So, keep that same energy you have, knowing you are safe with me, as when I am not around."

"I try to be brave," I said. "But it is hard for me when times get rough." I sighed, hoping he would sympathize with me.

"When times get rough," he said confidently. "You must trust that you are safe and can overcome obstacles that get in your way. I know a lot is happening in our neighborhood, but you can rest assured that you have nothing to fear. It concerns me that you worry so much at your age," he said. "Try to relax. You have no control over the madness in this world, and it is not worth stressing over. Besides, all areas have issues."

I think about what my dad is saying, but I also think about moving somewhere nicer. When my mom watches her favorite television series, the communities the characters live in are beautiful. The houses are enormous and far apart, have pools and fancy cars, and everything is peaceful. I want to live in a place like that. The characters all look happy and worry-free. I bet they do not lose sleep hearing loud music and people out partying at all times of night.

"So if we move somewhere else, there will be issues, but we will be alright. Right?" I asked.

"Of course!" he answered, "But that doesn't mean we should move though," he laughed.

"Why not?", I asked sounding defeated.

"Maybe if we were somewhere else, the issues won't be as bad," I suggested.

"I know what is best for you," he said.

Just then, there was a tug on my dad's line. He pulled and pulled, but the tugging did not last long at all. Whatever was tugging at the end of his line was determined to get away and it broke free.

"I guess he wasn't having it today," my dad said as he chuckled. "He was determined to be free, and he got what he wanted," he said. "That fish can be a good example for you." he said.

"How can the fish be a good example for me?" I asked.

"Well," he said as he relaxed his pole and looked at me. "You have to be determined to be free like that fish. No matter what situation you are in, you should persevere until you see that things are all good."

"I never said I didn't feel free. I just don't like living here and I think we should move." I said.

"How can you feel free when you constantly have a fear of everything?" he asked.

"I'm not afraid of everything." I said as I tried to sound confident. "Just some things or maybe just a few things. Yeah, just a few things", I said.

"Ok, if you say so. But even a little fear takes away your freedom", Dad said.

I was beginning to feel more and more like that fish. Even though he fought for his freedom from the hook, he was still stuck in the pond. There was no way out for him. No stream leading into a larger more beautiful body of water. He was stuck in the same murky pond that he was born in. He may be free from my dad's line, but he is not free from his living environment. Just like me.

Chapter 3

Confronting the Beast

Time passed slowly, and we waited patiently for
fish to bite our enticing worms. It was quiet. My
dad's music blended in with the white noise at the
pond. Suddenly, things became uncomfortable for
me. I sensed something stirring. I tried to avoid the
awkward feeling with all my might, but it was hard
to ignore. I knew it was the beast. It's been here
with us before, but I am usually the only one that is
aware of its presence. I never know what to expect
when it is here; sometimes it comes and goes but it
is so unpredictable. The beast's growl started
quietly, but it did not take long to get into full beast
mode. I am sure you think I must be terrified since
my dad thinks I am afraid of everything, but I am
not afraid. I was the only one who heard the beast at
first, but now it was apparent my dad had heard it
too.

My dad looked away from the pond briefly

to explore the sound, but he quickly went back to fishing. I, on the other hand, could not ignore the beast. The beast was determined to be recognized as its growl grew longer and louder. I remained calm and refused to be moved, although I knew the beast would surface soon. I stood my ground as I bravely waited and tried not to be distracted.

Suddenly, a sizeable bellowing sound reverberated through the park, catching me and my dad off guard.

"Is that your stomach growling like that?" he asked me in astonishment.

"Yep! It absolutely is." I answered, trying hard to hold in my laugh.

Still amazed by the loud grumble, my dad told me to put my fishing handle in the holder and get something to eat. It was still early, and although I had just had breakfast, that beast of a growl from my stomach let me know I could not wait for lunchtime to get something to eat. Grabbing the hand sanitizer and pulling out several moist towels, I could not clean my hands enough. My hands still felt yucky after cutting the live bait, no matter how much I wiped them. My stomach was demanding, and the beast would not be ignored. The beast had to be tamed, and I had to be the one to tame it. I looked through all the goodies my mom packed for us. She usually packs the same thing for both of us, but Dad's sandwiches have an extra layer of everything. She filled our bags with something from each food group, and I usually don't finish all my food, but Dad does. However, today will be different because the beast wants a big meal, and I will give it to him.

I grabbed a sandwich and some chips and sat in my chair near my dad.

"It is not time for a break, so don't get too comfortable," my dad insisted. "We might get some big ones to take the bait, so eat up," he said as he rested his rod and felt the muscles in my upper arm. Next, he flexed the muscles in his tattooed arms. "You will need all the energy and strength you have if we get a big one," he said as he looked at my arms. "Besides, I don't want your growling stomach to scare off the fish, so fill up!"

We have a set time for our lunch break, and my stomach usually knows when that is. It felt weird eating so early and breaking away from our routine. Rushing through breakfast probably tricked my body into thinking I was full when I wasn't, but oh boy, my body reminded me that I was still hungry. I thought about how loud my stomach was and started laughing again. A few bites of my sandwich and chips put the beast in its place. The growls and rumbles slowly started to settle in my stomach. Finally, the beast in my belly calmed down, and everything was awkwardly quiet.

The quiet time was abruptly interrupted when police cars zipped down the streets with their sirens blaring. The cars were moving fast and getting closer. I stood up to see where they were going. I was glad to see them quickly race away from where we were, although I wondered what was happening.

"It's always something," I said under my breath.

My dad just sat there. He did not flinch. He acted as though he did not hear a thing. How could he be so calm and focused? Was fishing so important that nothing else in the world mattered? It is barely the crack of dawn, and already there is chaos.

I was enjoying my early lunch until all the chaos with the sirens blaring. I was glad finishing my sandwich and chips did not take long because all the action with the police cars ruined my appetite. I wiped my mouth and hands and reluctantly grabbed my rod.

"This neighborhood is too rough for me," I mumbled as I covered my ears to block the loud, wailing sounds of the sirens from another police car that was approaching.

"Are you done eating?" my dad asked.

"Those sirens bother me," I grumbled without answering my dad. "I hear them in the morning and at night. There is always something going on here. How can you possibly like it here and think it is safe?" I asked, grabbing my pole from the holder. I pretended to focus on my fishing line, but I couldn't help wondering what was happening.

"The sirens don't bother me," he responded. "I mean, I'm concerned for those in need of help and those on their way to help them, but I just don't let it bother me, and you shouldn't either." He reached over to pat me on the back and continued, "If you let every siren or situation bother you, you will be a nutcase before you're grown. You will have control over some things in your life and some things you won't. Focus on what you can control, and don't let the other stuff bother or distract you," he said.

"There are so many things I can't control," I said. "Bad things happen all the time. How will I know what I can control?" I said as I placed my fishing rod in the holder and looked at my dad.

"Look," he said as he turned to me and placed his fishing rod in his holder. "Life is full of ups and downs. There will always be crime, sickness, difficulties, and pain, but you must consider how to prevent or at least avoid them. Crime is tricky, but you can stay aware of your surroundings and avoid getting involved with people who are looking for trouble. You can avoid being sick by keeping yourself healthy and eating right. Most of all, you know your mom and I are always here for you." he concluded.

I sat down and watched the water as I tugged on the line. I wondered what my dad was thinking about, but I did not have the nerve to ask. He stood up, stretched, and put his fishing pole in the holder, yawning. Soon after, I stretched and let out an even more enormous yawn.

"Are you bored?" my dad asked me.

"No way. I only yawned because you yawned. Yawning is contagious, you know?" I asked as I looked at him and smiled.

"So, that's what they say." He placed his rod's handle in the holder and sat beside me.

"If yawning is contagious, what made me yawn?" he asked. "When I yawned earlier, I did not hear you return the yawn. Does that mean yawning is selectively contagious?" I can see he is in a playful mood. Occasionally, he asks me silly questions to get a reaction from me and challenge my thinking skills. I try to be as intellectual as possible at those times, but I turn to humor when I can't be. I stretched my arms and faked a yawn, saying, "Fishing isn't boring to me, Dad, but talking about yawning is?" I snickered and pretended to be bored.

"Oh, you got jokes now?" he said as he leaped from his chair to grab me, but I'm stealthy. Even with my rod still in my hand, I jumped up and out moved him. He looks proud to see how skillfully I avoided his reach.

"You can't catch me!" putting the rod down, I laughed as I dodged him again.

"You're pretty fast for a little dude! Perhaps we can take a break to see how fast you are in a quick race," he said as he stretched.

Chapter 4

Win, Lose or Draw

We rested our poles in the holder and headed to the closest tree to prepare to race. The tree is old, but it is solid. Although it is huge, it looks like a gentle giant. The sun shines on it, and its leaves protect us with cooling shade. The park is quiet, and the pond is motionless. You will never find grass greener than the grass that grows here, or the aroma of the flowers more fragrant. You would think this was the most beautiful place in the world, but it is not. The trees hold a secret, and their shade protects the secret from anyone who tries to figure it out.

The trees do not fool me. As I get closer to the biggest and tallest tree in the park, I try to look for clues. Clues that will lead me to the biggest secret of the park. The secret that my dad has access to but has built an alliance with the trees and has vowed not to tell. The secret I have been trying to learn all my long nine years of living. Or at least two of those nine long years.

You see, my dad had a childhood friend named Xavier who used to play by these trees with him, and it was by one of these trees that Xavier became a victim of gum violence. I have always imagined that this huge tree is the tree where he was shot and killed. Just the thought of it haunts me every time I see it. No matter how beautiful people think the tree is, I only see the darkness of the secret it protects.

I know you must be wondering how I know about this awful secret if it is so protected. There is no secret to that so let me explain. One day, I was walking past my parent's room while throwing my ball in the air. I do not know how it happened, but I dropped the ball. That never happens because I am a very skilled catcher. The ball rolled into their room and under their bed. Since the ball was out of my reach, I had to look at all the boxes under the bed. It was not my fault that I had to open one of the boxes to make sure the ball did not damage anything in it.

The box had lots of photos, and I felt obligated to look at each one. There were pictures of my dad and his childhood best friend Xavier. They were at the park, in school performances, at my grandmother's house, and many other places. There was an obituary with a picture of Xavier on it. Under it was a picture of a tree like this one. The tree's trunk was adorned with flowers, candles, teddy bears, and a big picture of a Xavier. I never asked about the picture, in fact, I put everything back in the box, grabbed my ball and left my parents' room.

The closer I got to the tree, the less I felt like racing my dad. I had so many questions for my dad, but I did not want to a Donnie Downer, so I tried to think of fun things about the tree. My dad loves sharing stories about Xavier, but he also enjoys telling stories about him and my mom. I especially like the story about how my mom and dad were allergic to one another. My dad said he always thought she was cute when they were in school, but she was gross because she was a girl. He did not have time for girls, but he and his friends had plenty of time to play ball, sneak into movie theaters, and go fishing. It was not until high school that he realized my mother was not gross, and he did not have an allergic reaction to her. By then, everything had changed. He did not have time for his friends because he wanted to spend all his time with my mom.

At the tree, my dad pumped himself up and tried to intimidate me.

"You sure you want to do this?" he asked. "You know I'll give you a head start, but I'm not going to pity you just because you're a kid."

"I'm good," I said as I stared at the tree. "I won't need a head start," I replied, regretting saying it as soon as it slipped out of my mouth.

My dad loves a good challenge as much as he loves fishing. I was charged and ready to race him until we got to the tree. It baffles me how he acts as though it is just a regular tree with no significance. I know that what happened to his friend occurred long ago, but you just don't forget things like that. I wondered if he had forgotten what had happened.

"We can start here and go to the rock at the end of the field house. I'll wait for you there when I win," my dad laughed as he pointed to the rock.

"I'll be there first, so why don't you grab a water bottle and hand it to me when you finally finish the race?" I said, even though I knew I could not beat him yet. "I'll start the race," I said as we leaned into position. "Ready? Get set…" I started, but noisy sirens filled the air before I could say go. "Stop! Stop! Stop!" I yelled as I watched the swift police cars zoom by. "Let's wait for them to pass." I said.

"Are you stalling?" Dad asked. "I told you I would give you a head start."

"I don't need a head start," I mumbled. "I just need to be able to concentrate. Besides, I don't want to run while the police are around," I said in an annoyed tone. "What if they think we are running from them? Or what if they think we did something wrong?" I stopped asking questions because I did not want to know the answers.

My dad looked at me and threw his hands up

and grabbed his head and asked, "Are you serious right now?"

We watched the noisy cars race off until we could no longer see or hear them. Then, my dad looked back at me. I knew he was frustrated but I had valid concerns.

"You watch too much television!" he said. "Stop thinking the worse about everything."

One last police car came blaring down the street with noisy sirens. I covered my ears and watched the police car race down the street. Although the cars were gone and the loud sirens had stopped, I no longer wanted to run. Not just because I knew I would lose, but because I was no longer in the mood for a father-son footrace. I slowly headed back to our fishing spot.

"Are you giving up already?" Dad asked.

"I'm not giving up. I just don't want to race anymore. Maybe we can race before we leave." I answered without giving him eye contact.

"Have it your way, but I will consider this a draw if we don't race later. I win by default," he said.

That was his way of challenging me, and it usually worked. However, I could not focus on racing right now. I was too busy concerning myself with what was going on with all that police action so early in the morning.

We quietly walked back to where our fishing poles were resting in the holders. I heard my dad take a deep breath as he picked up a smooth stone. He played with the stone in his hand before he tossed it out to the pond far away from where our floaters were bobbing. It's always cool to see how his stones skip on top of the water.

"You know," he said as he tapped me on the shoulder to get my attention. "You worry too much." He grabbed his fishing rod from the holder and walked to the water's edge. "I think you are afraid of things you should not be afraid of." I joined him at the edge of the water. He was preparing a lecture for me. I am usually not

enthused about hearing his speeches, but this was
the perfect opportunity to ask uncomfortable
questions.

"How can you be so calm about everything
all the time?" I asked before he could start with his
lecture. "Nothing ever seems to bother you."

My dad pretended to have a collar on his T-
shirt, and he tugged at it confidently and said, "It's
just what I do." He winked at me and laughed as he
continued. "I learned long ago that things will
happen in our lives that we cannot control. No
matter what happens, we only have control over our
actions. People will do what they do, and you can't
control that." he sighed. "You asked me if I feel
safe living here, and I do," he said after a brief
silence. "That does not mean I am not concerned
about what happens here or that I don't care. It is
just the opposite. I care deeply about this
neighborhood and the people that live here.
Unfortunately, we cannot afford to move, but I still
wouldn't want to even if we could." He looked as
though he was not interested in fishing anymore as

he looked at me and continued. "I want things to get better for us all, but running away and moving to another neighborhood will not help make things better for anyone. All communities have issues, and not one is perfect."

"I see perfect places on tv and in movies," I said. "Can't we find a place like those to move to?" I asked, hoping he would consider my plea.

"The truth is," he said as he put his pole down, turned, and faced me. "There are no perfect neighborhoods because people live in neighborhoods. People are not perfect, and you must remember that. People don't always make good choices, and sometimes they make really poor decisions," he said and then quickly corrected himself, "No! Not sometimes, a lot of times." He stretched as he looked at me for a response or a reaction. "I love it here. I think I would feel safer here than in a neighborhood that does not welcome me with open arms or an open mind." He grabbed me and gave me a tight squeeze. "You can't possibly understand this at your age, but there will come a time when you know exactly what I mean.

Dad's lectures usually include stories from his childhood and start with, "when I was your age." But this lecture was different. He did not remind me how good I have it compared to when he was a child. Nor did it last for over an hour or so. But since he did not bring up his childhood, I thought maybe I should. I did not know how to start the conversation, but I knew that this would be the perfect time to ask what happened to Xavier.

Now it is just as good a time as any, and as soon as he picks up his fishing rod, I'm going to ask him about Xavier. No, I will ask him as soon as he blinks his eyes or stretches. Or maybe it would be best if he starts to talk about something and then I change the subject and ask him. I am so ready for this. Dad thinks I am afraid of everything, well I will just have to show him that I am not afraid to ask about Xavier. That's right! The time is now! I want answers and he will have to give them to me. I'll show him who's scared. Then again, maybe I should wait until we come back another Saturday.

Chapter 5

The Catch

As the morning sun shone brighter and hotter, we sat quietly in our chairs, watching and waiting for fish to get caught on our lines. By now, more people have arrived at the pond. I glanced at a family setting up their fishing spot, and before I knew it, I felt a tug at my line. The floater was bobbing wildly. I gripped the handle of my fishing pole tightly and pulled at it. For every strong pull I made, the thing on the end of the line created an even more brutal force. My dad did not let go of his line to help me; instead, he coached my every move.

"I think he's on there good," he cheered. "Reel 'em in, and don't let go!" he exclaimed. If only it were that easy.

"I'm trying, Dad!" I cried. "He's so strong. Help me. Help me please!" I begged.

"You got this, he laughed. So just hang in there and don't let go," Dad said.

"I see him! I see him!" I yelled as I watched the fish jump in and out of the water.

"Don't get too excited, or you'll let him get away!" he said as he slowly walked over to me.

I was able to see how big the fish was. He was big, but his pull was more extensive than his size. I was determined to make the catch on my own, but I knew I would need reinforcement from my dad. I started reeling the fish in, but he was stubborn. He swam away, still connected to my line. I pulled him toward me with all my might. Finally, I moved closer to the water. My footing was uneven, so I knelt on one knee for better balance.

"He's getting tired now!" my dad yelled excitedly.

"So am I!" I yelled, ready to let go.

"He's yours, man!" dad said reassuringly. "How bad do you want him?" he asked.

I wanted him badly, but the determined fish wanted his freedom more than I wanted a fish dinner.

After what felt like hours, I pulled at my line fiercely and backed away from the water. The tired fish was about to give up, but he soon got a second wind. Finally, he jerked on the line, and I nearly dropped it.

I saw my dad reach for me, but then he stepped away. "Almost there." he continued to cheer.

"I got him, Dad," I claimed. "He's right…

where…I … want … him!" I said, reaching to grab him as he hung in the air at the end of my line.

I managed to pull him close to me as he indignantly wiggled. He was a nice size, not too big and not too small. He was just right. It was my first catch of the day, and I was thrilled. As much as I wanted my dad to help me with the fish, I was proud knowing that I caught it and reeled it in by myself.

"Nice catch," my dad said as he proudly looked at me. "That's a brown trout. He's roughly three or four pounds," he said with his biggest smile. "Go ahead and put him in the bucket." He grabbed my fishing rod as I removed the trout from the hook. I could tell he was proud of me. "Look at my little angler," he said as he palmed my head and shook it. "It's about time these fish started waking up. The next one is going to be mine, and I guarantee you; it's going to be even larger than yours," he vowed.

The trout was annoyed as I took the hook from his mouth. It squirmed and danced around in my hands until he finally wore out. I could not wait to get him out of my hands. I put him in the bucket and could still hear him flopping around. I felt sorry for the little fellow, but at the same time, I felt proud knowing my dad was pleased with me.

There were more people at the pond; some were fishing. Others were jogging, walking, skipping stones, or just enjoying the area's beauty. The park is in the center of a big grassy area with several benches. It has walk and bike paths around the pond and the field house. I saw our neighbor, Mr. Johnson, walking on the trail, heading our way.

As Mr. Johnson approached us, my dad put his fishing pole in the holder and stood up to shake his hand and greet him.

"Good morning, Mr. Johnson," I yelled over my shoulder to speak to him.

"What's up, Jamal?" he responded.

"I caught a fish!" I boasted.

"Is that right?" he asked coming closer to

see the fish. "Now catch one for me," he said playfully.

Mr. Johnson headed back over to my dad, and they began to chat.

"Did you hear those gunshots last night? They sounded really close, and I could barely sleep." Mr. Johnson said.

I knew what Mr. Johnson was talking about because it was impossible not to hear the shots fired. I held my fishing rod tight as the floater sat on the water. At that moment, I was fishing, but not for fish. Instead, I was curious about how my dad would answer the question, so I was fishing for information. My dad does not approve of children minding grown folks' business, but I needed to know how he was going to respond to see if it would help me convince him to move us away from here.

"I heard the shots," dad answered, "and I went to sleep. I can't lose sleep over every shot fired in our neighborhood. I knew I had to get out here early," my dad said. "It's my duty to see that no fish is left behind," he chuckled and gave our neighbor a nudge. Mr. Johnson snickered, but his snicker was short-lived because he took the situation more seriously than my dad did.

"I'm getting out of here as soon as possible. I'm taking my family to the burbs the first chance I get." Mr. Johnson said in a stern voice.

I pretended to be engrossed in fishing, but I was not thinking about the fish. I could not convince my dad to move us away from here, but perhaps Mr. Johnson could.

"Man, have fun looking for a place," my dad said. "We aren't going anywhere. I'm staying right here with my family."

There it is. I got my hopes up for nothing.

Mr. Johnson looked at my dad with disappointment. "How can you stay here?" he asked. "Nearly every night, we hear gunshots. Our children deserve better!" he said as he pointed at me, then going back and forth with his pointer finger pointing at my dad and then to himself. "We deserve better!" Mr. Johnson stormed off.

My dad was not phased. He offered no explanation defending his choice to stay here.

My dad started walking toward me and I pretended not to hear anything they talked about. I wiggled my pole and watched the water intently pretending to be engaged in fishing, but curiosity got the best of me.

"I heard the gunshots he was talking about," I blurted out as I watched my dad settle back into his chair and grab his fishing rod. I thought my dad would be upset that I listened to grown folks' business, but I am sure he realized I could not help but hear the conversation. Afterall, it was not my fault that Mr. Johnson was talking loudly. I waited for my dad to respond. Instead, he grabbed two water bottles from our lunch bag. He leaned over and handed me one, and he kept one for himself.

"I heard the shots Mr. Johnson was talking about," I said as I reached to get the water. Then I continued, "I bet when Mr. Johnson moves his family to the suburbs, they will not hear gunshots anymore,"

My dad took a sip and put the cap back on his bottle. "Look at all the people moving out of the neighborhood. They are not just leaving their homes. They are leaving the community, schools, life-long friends, and everything, but they don't see the value in our neighborhood. The richness of our bond as a community. Mr. Johnson sees the chaos and trouble in our neighborhood because he looks for it. He expects it," he said. "Not me, though. I keep my eyes on the prize. I stay focused and on top of what's really going on around me, and you should do the same." He said and grabbed his water bottle and started drinking the water again.

I had no words. Eyes on what prize? What is he talking about? He can't possibly believe that living here is a prize. Can't he see that everybody is moving out? Well, everybody but us and the troublemakers. I came here thinking I would get answers to questions about Xavier and convince my dad to move out of the neighborhood, but now I am even more confused and do not have any answers.

"Guess what, Jamal," Dad said as he jumped

and moved to the water's edge.

Something was tugging at his line. My dad gripped his rod tightly as the rod was being pulled farther away from him. The floater was dancing ferociously at the surface of the water. There were splashes and ripples under his line. There was something big on that hook. He struggled as he began to reel the fish in. We saw the fish jump out of the water as he pulled the line. It was another brown trout, only this one was huge.

"You got 'em, Dad," I yelled. Now, I was the hype man. "Show him who's the boss!" I laughed as I pumped him up.

"I got 'em, Jamal!" Dad said confidently, not breaking a sweat.

"He's huge!" I yelled.

"Yes. He. Is. But I got 'em!" he said as he cranked his reel ferociously and yanked the fish out of the water.

Chapter 6

Snitches Give Stitches

The park was getting busier as more people came to fish. I was ready to go home but didn't know how to tell my dad. We sat quietly, looking out at the pond.

"Have I ever told you I had to be in the house before the street lights came on?" My dad asked me out of the blue. "My parents did not want me outside when it got dark," he said as he reminisced on his past. "It wasn't just my parents that made their children come into the house before the street lights came on. Nope! Every child on our block would make a beeline for their front door as soon as the street lights started flicking. No child was in sight when the lights were completely on."

I remembered the story, but his timing was strange to me. I put my rod in the holder and examined his catch.

"Yes, dad," I answered. "You told me you had to be in the house before the street lights came on. But why?" I asked as I looked at the fish.

"Are you asking why we had to be in the house before the streetlights were on, or why I'm asking you this?" he asked.

"I guess both," I answered.

"Fair enough," my dad said, placing his fishing rod in the holder. "I was asking because I was making an observation, but maybe we can talk about it briefly," he answered. "We had to be in the house before the streetlights came on for our safety." After taking a deep breath, he continued. "When I was a kid, we did everything outside, even on the coldest days of winter. Now, you and your buddies barely spend any time outside. It's all about video games and social media. For us, our social media was getting outside, being social, and playing as many games we could fit into the few hours we were out there," he said as he sat in his chair. He looked over his shoulder to where our food was.

"Do you think this is a good time to take a lunch break?" he asked.

I shook my head to gesture yes. But then, I quickly remembered how much my dad detests when I answer questions with a motion, even though he always does it.

"Sure!" I answered. I wasn't hungry, but I was tired of fishing. We stood up and stretched. It felt like we had been sitting for several hours. The field house is too far to walk to wash our hands, so my mom packs cleansing wipes with our lunches. Unfortunately, my hands still felt dirty from earlier when I had put the worms on the line.

My dad spread out a blanket and grabbed our snacks and sandwiches. Neither of us was ready to sit down again after sitting for so long, but we stretched a couple more times and got comfortable on the blanket to eat our lunch. I was hoping I would not have to remind my dad that we were in the middle of a conversation, but he was really into that sandwich. I knew I would have to remind him that we were talking about his good old days.

"Didn't you have video games when you were a kid?" I asked to get him back on the topic.

"Of course, but not high-tech ones like the games you all have now. But they were fun," Dad said, shaking his head. "Oh, and don't get me wrong, I'm not knocking your video games and social media stuff", he said as he bit into his sandwich. "I just don't understand how they can compete with the great outdoors. You know, real reality stuff, like tag and it or hide-and-seek. The REAL fun stuff."

He and my mom do not allow me to spend

more than an hour a day on my devices during the school week, and between basketball, soccer, church, and family time, I barely get a couple of hours on the weekend.

"I don't like going outside because it's rough out there. The craziness may have started at night when you were a kid, but for us, it's a 24-hour thing. It's never safe during the day or night." I said, hoping he would want to talk more so we wouldn't have to return to fishing. My dad was plucking grapes and popping them in his mouth, and I couldn't tell if he was considering what I said.

"Don't get me wrong," he said after swallowing a mouthful of grapes, "I never said things weren't crazy during the day. They were, but as kids, we minded our kid-business and didn't get involved in the nonsense some of the other kids would get involved in. We had nosey neighbors watching us," he laughed. "Well, I guess you can say, concerned neighbors. They weren't exactly nosey. They were just looking out for us. The gang members didn't stand a chance at recruiting any of us because everybody knew everybody's mamas and daddies, and they talked all the time. They constantly snitched on us when we got out of line. In those days, snitches did not get stitches; they gave them," he laughed. After popping the last few grapes into his mouth, he pulled his trash together. I knew this meant he was ready to get back to fishing.

I gathered my wrappers and what was left from my lunch and prepared myself for more fishing.

"I'm glad we don't have people getting in our business like you had," I said.

"I'm glad we did. Maybe I did not appreciate it then, but I sure do now. It's too bad there aren't more neighbors that get involved with what goes on in the neighborhood. Maybe then you and your friends would get outdoors more and experience more than just video games," Dad said as he picked up his rod. "The world's nosiest neighbor lived next to us," he said. "We called her Ms. Jan, and Ms. Jan didn't play. She would smack our bottoms if we did anything out of order. Then she would tell our parents everything," he chuckled, "things were different back then. If we misbehaved, she corrected us."

I could tell my dad was having an emotional moment. He was no longer looking out at the pond. Instead, his head hung down, and he hesitated before he continued. "Our parents disciplined us with love, and we respected them because we knew they cared about us. Some kids nowadays have no guidance or discipline and don't respect their parents, others, or themselves. So, nobody wants to get involved in what the youth are doing anymore. Our neighborhood was a village. An African proverb says It takes the whole village..." I jumped in to join him, and we recited the rest together, "to raise a child," we said as we chuckled. He smiled to show his approval that I remembered what he had taught me, and then he continued to speak, "This society has taken neighbors out of our neighborhood, and without neighbors, it is no longer a neighborhood. It's just the hood." My dad glanced at me and gestured for me to wrap it up so we could return to fishing.

"So, you felt safe as a child because someone was always watching over you and your friends?" I asked as I watched him look at me and put our garbage in a bag.

"Absolutely!" he asserted. "I feel safe even now with all the rough stuff going on. I must be here for my family, and that's enough to keep me going," he said boldly.

Chapter 7

Processions and Protection

I headed to the garbage bin to throw away the waste from our lunch, and I saw a squirrel sitting on top of the garbage lid. The squirrel cautiously sat and watched me as I approached. The closer I got to the bin, the more the squirrel became territorial. It was almost as if he were guarding the garbage bin and daring me to get near it. I accepted his challenge and chased after him with a big scary growl. I sounded like a deranged maniac, but the squirrel took his time leaving the garbage bin. He was more annoyed than frightened by me.

As I disposed of our trash, I saw what I thought was a parade coming up the street. There was a policeman on a motorcycle heading a trail of cars. The siren was off, but the lights flashed, and he was going super slow. There was no music playing, and there were no floats. I soon realized that it was not a parade.

"Dad," I called out. "Can I get a closer look at those cars?"

"Why do you want to watch a funeral procession?" he asked.

"Who died?" I asked, looking at my dad as I waited for him to answer.

"I have no idea." He said in a low baffled voice.

We watched the cars go by slowly. There had to be at least thirty or more cars. More police drove on the side of some vehicles, and one blocked the intersection when the traffic light changed.

"It must be someone super important, right, dad?" I asked as I looked at the people in the cars. Some were still mourning, and others were talking and laughing.

"Well, everyone is important," he said as he picked up a stick and pulled off the bark. Throwing the stick toward the pond, he tugged at my shirt, and we headed back to our spot. I followed him, but I kept looking back at the procession. When the last car passed, we were back in our area. We grabbed our rods and walked closer to the water's edge.

"I know everyone is important, but not everyone gets a police escort for their funeral, so what made that person so special?" I asked.

"How did I know you wouldn't let this go?" Dad asked, shaking his head. "Well, if the deceased was involved in gang activity, the family may need protection in case there is any retaliation."

"What makes you think it was something to do with a gang?" I asked him."

"Well," he hesitated. "Lately, there's been a lot of retaliation with gang members, so police escort the family members for their safety. Just in case a rival gang gets any crazy ideas," he said while shaking his head. But, of course, if someone died from sickness or old age, the police would not have had to be there."

"Oh, I see," I murmured, wishing I had never asked.

"Now, don't let that frighten you more," Dad said, rolling his eyes. "It's up to you to make good and wise choices and not get involved with kids that make trouble."

We never talk about this, although it is always on my mind. This is the conversation that will open the door for me to ask about Xavier, instead of talking about sports and school and girls. I never want to talk about girls. It does not make sense to talk about girls. My dad thinks he saw me looking at a girl in church and he assumed I liked her. Most of the time, I'm not looking at her, I am looking past her, and it seems like I'm looking at her, but I'm not. Her name is Dymond, and I guess she's alright. I wouldn't know because I have never paid attention to her long enough to know or care.

Dymond goes to my school, and she is good at everything. She plays basketball and dominates the court. Dymond is in my science group, and when I accidentally knocked over the class rat's cage, and he escaped, she was the only one that didn't run away screaming like the rest of us. Instead, she calmly went into the storage room and pulled the rat out.

Her face shines when she smiles, and I am

almost sure I hear harmonious music when she speaks. When Dymond is absent from school, it makes the day drag. I don't know why, but I look for her every day at school and church on Sundays.

"Have you heard anything I've said?" my dad asked annoyed.

"I'm sorry. Wait, what?" I asked, snapping out of my daydream.

"You always seem so curious about Xavier, and now you aren't even listening to me talk about what happened to him!" he said. "What are you over there thinking about?" he asked.

There was no way I would tell him I was thinking about Dymond. My goal today was to get him to talk about Xavier, and here I am, stuck on thoughts about Dymond.

"No, I was just, just… wait, what did you say happened to him?" I searched his face to see if he had already said how Xavier died, but it was hard to tell.

"Xavier and I would play outside every day. We would come here and skip stones, catch tadpoles, climb trees, race, and do all kinds of crazy things. One day while we were playing, we both got stung by a bee. Can you believe it? We both got stung on the same day around the same time. He was the first to get stung. We were skipping stones, and he picked up a stone close to a flower. A bee came off that flower and charged Xavier as if he owed him money. I saw the whole thing, but I couldn't help him because, at the same time, there must have been another bee nearby that did not appreciate us being there. He buzzed in my face, and I gave him a big swat. Before I knew it, he had landed on my hand, giving me a taste of his stinger. After that, we both ran around the pond like two crybabies." he said as he returned to tending to his fishing rod.

As fascinating as his bee story was, I did not want to hear it. Xavier did not die from a bee sting. We were about twenty feet away from where someone shot and killed his best friend years ago, and my dad was talking about bees. I thought we were making progress, but I guess we were not. I decided I would have to get right to it if I wanted to know what happened.

"Why did someone shoot Xavier?" I asked abruptly.

"We've been here all morning and have two great fish to show for it," he said. "Perhaps our next trip will bring more success. Let's start wrapping things up," he huffed as he pulled his line out of the water.

He's not one to change the subject often, but I fell for it, and before I knew it, I forgot about my question and packed up to leave the pond.

Chapter 8

Un-bee-lievable Truths

My parents make an ordinary fish fry into a neighborhood feast on days like this. We always have plenty of food for whoever smells the grill and decides to join us. I could already taste my mom's food, and she hadn't lit the charcoals yet. It would be another ten to fifteen minutes before we made it home, so my dad whipped out his phone and called mom to tell her she should start preparing the grill.

We did not have a lot of fish, but my mom was thawing out fish, ground beef, and sausages before we went fishing.

While strolling in the hot sun, I continued our conversation about Xavier. I tried to sound serious, so my dad would take me seriously.

"Dad, I know it is hard for you to talk about Xavier, but perhaps talking about it is what you need to do to have closure," I said in an intense voice. "Let's talk about Xavier."

The pep in my dad's step was gone as he came to a complete stop. He put down his things and covered his face with both hands. Oh no, I was not expecting him to get emotional. I think I went too far this time. I should have left well enough alone. I stopped to put my things down and comfort my dad, but he bellowed a loud hysterical laugh before I could.

"Oh, my goodness, oh my goodness!" He said as he chuckled. "You are hilarious! Where did you get that from, one of your mom's talk shows?" He started picking his things up as he continued to laugh hysterically. "Wait 'til I tell your mom."

I failed to see the humor in all this but seeing him laugh like this was funny. Usually, my mom is the only person who can get a laugh like this out of him.

"Dad, I'm so serious. I really want to know. Please tell me!" I said in my normal voice to avoid another outburst.

"I'm sorry," he said as we continued to walk home. "I know you are being serious. It's just that you sounded like a talk show host. I know Xavier's death is nothing to laugh at, but even he would have got a laugh out of how you said that" he said as he pulled himself together. "I don't know, Jamal. The world could use more people they can talk to and trust. Then maybe things won't be as bad as they are. Maybe that's your calling, Jamal." he said as he grabbed me by the top of my head and shook it gently. "Maybe you will be a therapist one day. You certainly are a good listener when you're not daydreaming."

I never thought of myself as a therapist. I

have always pictured myself as a private investigator. I like getting the facts and solving mysteries, but therapists do that too. As we approached the park's play area, we saw families with their children and people walking dogs.

"Okay," dad said, "I know you are curious about this, but you worry too much at your age. I'm not sure how you will handle it." He pointed at a bench in the park, "Let's sit down for a minute and see if you are ready to know the truth about his death," Dad said.

"After Xavier got stung by the bee…" he started.

"Dad! Not the bee story again." I interrupted.

"Don't interrupt," he said as he continued. "We were both in a lot of pain. His house was close, so we went there to get help. His grandmother was at the house, and she took care of us. She slapped honey on his face and my hand while making a baking soda paste." He paused as he looked at his hand where the bee had stung him years ago. "It was crazy. The honey made us feel better fast," he chuckled.

"Dad, please!" I blurted out. The suspense was too much.

"As I was saying," dad said as he continued, "while his grandma stirred the baking soda and water together, she glared at us. She thought we provoked the bees, but we were innocent. I told her we were skipping stones and that a bee was next to one of the stones Xavier picked up, and that's when the bee attacked him. I told her that another bee had come from nowhere and stung me. Xavier had been stung in the face and was in a lot of pain. His face and eyes were red and puffy."

"Was he allergic to bees?" I asked.

"No. I don't think so. His grandmother was very old fashioned and used tried and true remedies for everything," he said. "Anyway, Xavier claimed that it was the same bee that stung us both. I was certain we were stung by honey bees. Honey bees lose their stingers after they sting you." my dad cleared his throat before continuing. "Xavier got so mad at me," he continued. "He kept telling his grandmother it was the same bee, and when I disagreed, we argued back and forth until his grandmother shut us both up. I didn't care if it was one bee or two. I just knew it hurt," he looked at me and chuckled, "I was glad that no one saw us hopping around like we were crazy."

"Did Xavier heal quickly from the sting?" I asked, even though I just wanted to know how he died.

"Oh yeah, his physical scars went away after a couple of days, but not his emotional scars. They lasted much longer. Xavier was furious with me. His face stayed swollen for a few days, and he did not want anyone to see him. I, on the other hand, was outside playing every day. He was angry at me and wouldn't let me visit him. I never understood why he was so unforgiving. Truthfully, I didn't feel like I did anything to have to be forgiven for," he hung his head low and sighed. "Xavier distanced himself from me after that," he continued. "He wouldn't return my calls or speak to me when we saw each other outside." He shook his head and looked at me in disbelief. "We always argued and fought when I would lose a race and accuse him of cheating or when he would arrange the card deck so he would get all the winning cards, but we always remained close and moved on. Who would think something so silly would destroy our friendship?" He asked as he looked at me as if I had an answer.

"And then what happened?" I asked, anxious to hear more.

"Xavier's started hanging out with a new group of friends, most of which were older than he," he said as he inhaled loudly. "These new friends were always up to no good. They started fights and stole things from stores in the neighborhood. Xavier didn't know much about that life and wasn't as tough as them. We wrestled occasionally, but I always got the best of him. He could never pin me down," he laughed. "One day, he and this new group of friends met at the pond and got into a scuffle with other boys. It got pretty ugly, and lots of the guys got hurt from fighting.

One of the older boys pulled out a gun and shot it. They say that Xavier tried to run behind a tree, but before he could reach it, he fell to the ground," he said emotionally. "None of his new friends called for help, nor did they try to help him. They were all cowards! Especially the shooter." he huffed. "I know you think your mom and I are strict, but one day you will understand why we must be."

We gathered our things and started walking again.

"I'm glad you shared the story about Xavier with me, dad. I'm sorry it made you sad."

"I knew I would have to share the story with you one day; I was never sure when it would be a good time." He said as he playfully tugged on my dreads.

"I'm glad the bad guys got what they deserved, though!" I declared. "Especially the one that shot Xavier!"

My dad looked at me and grabbed me by my shoulder, "I never said they were bad guys. I don't know anything about any of them. I just know they made a horrible mistake that caused many people a great deal of grief." My dad said as he shook his head and let my shoulder go.

What does he mean he never called them bad guys? He didn't have to because everybody knows bad people do bad things. So why is he defending them?

"They're bad guys, Dad, and there is no other way to look at it," I demanded.

"I'm not sure we have a say in that," he said. "Good people," he said, making air quotes with his fingers, "do bad things," he continued. "People are people, and none of us are perfect. We all make dumb choices in life. Then there are times when the so-called bad guys do good things. When I was a kid, a guy named Fred lived in our neighborhood. He was someone that was in and out of prison all the time. When he was out, most people knew to stay away from him. My mom would speak to him every time we passed him on the street. Sometimes he would speak back, and other times he would give her a look that confirmed he did not want to be bothered. I thought he was the meanest person in the world, a bad guy, " he said again with air quotes. "Until one day, my mom and I were walking from the store, and a kid on a bike grabbed my mother's purse. He pulled the purse away from her so hard that she fell, dropping the groceries. I was too small to help her. There were several other people around, and no one offered to help. I watched people walk right by us." He shook his head in disbelief. "Well," he continued, "Fred was nearby and saw what happened. He grabbed my mom's purse off the kid's arm as he rode past him. He roughed the thief up and warned him never to come around here again. Afterward, he came to help my mom and return her purse. He asked her if she was alright and gave me the groceries that fell out of the bag. She offered him a couple of dollars as a reward, but he refused. My mom insisted, and he reluctantly took the money. I could not believe my eyes, and it did not stop there. Fred took a portion of the money my mom gave him and gave it to a beggar on the street," he said, grabbing his head.

"We walked past that beggar every day and never offered him anything, although my mom would give him fruit or something small from our groceries, but never any money. But Fred, the bad guy, did what we should all be doing, helping each other out."

"Fred did that out of guilt, I bet," I said sarcastically.

"Maybe," my dad said with a smirk. "But it doesn't matter because he did it. He was kind to the needy. All those people around us, the good guys, did nothing. Nothing to help my mother and nothing to help the needy," he said again with air quotes.

"Hey, wait a minute, " I paused as I gave him a long hard look, "Whatever happened to the kid that shot Xavier?"

"No one ever came forward to report what happened." he calmly said as he checked on the fish hanging from the line we put them on. He waved his hand in front of his nose to show me that the fish had a foul odor. We both laughed. "Many people were at the pond that day. They talked about the shooting to one another, but when the police asked questions, no one had anything to say."

I could not believe what I was hearing. I jumped in front of my dad and held my hand up for him to stop like I was directing traffic.

"Wait, you mean to tell me that he got away with it?" I asked my dad as he passed me and continued walking. He laughed at my failed effort to try and stop him.

"Jamal, I never said he got away with it. I just said no one came forward to report the activity. The police never arrested anyone, but that doesn't mean he got away with it," he muttered. "No one ever gets away with things like that."

Chapter 9

Grilled Lessons

As we approached our house, I saw my mother standing in the doorway, smiling from ear to ear. My foot barely touched the porch before she greeted me with cheers and hugs. My dad had already told her about how I caught the fish without his help. I pretended it was no big deal and tried not to show any emotion, but I was proud of my catch, and it showed. While she squeezed the air out of me, I smiled uncontrollably. I finally caught a fish big enough for us to cook and eat, and I did it alone. My dad got more of the same as he dangled the fish in front of her.

It was just a little before noon, but the smell of burning charcoal was in the air. Every burner on the stove had a hot pot sitting on it. I dashed past my mom as she was peeling potatoes. I headed to the living room to play my favorite video game. It wouldn't be long before my cousins would be here, and I would have to take turns with them and share my video games. I wanted to use this time to brush up on my skills and play my games alone before my cousins arrived.

"Where do you think you're going, young man?" Mom asked.

There was lots of work to be done for the cookout, but I did my part when I caught the fish. I hoped my mom would remember that I put a lot into catching that fish and I should be rewarded. Besides, I have video game playing time on

Saturdays, and every minute counts, but I reminded her just in case.

"It's video game time. I will set the timer, so I won't exceed my limit." I answered.

"Hmm... nice try, but today we need all hands on deck. Your cousins will be here soon, and you won't have a limit on your video time once they get here. You will have plenty of time for games later. I need you in the kitchen," she said as she peeled potato after potato.

"Yes, ma'am," I sighed as I went to the sink to wash my hands. But then, I saw the fish I caught staring at me as it sat on a bed of ice. "Thanks for nothing," I whispered to the fish. I was excited to have my cousins visit, but I wanted some game time to myself. After all, my cousin Tony will make it a point to take over every game since he is the oldest of all the cousins. I probably won't even get a turn to play my games.

"Well, today is a great day to be a helper," My mom said as she pulled a list off the refrigerator. "Today, you can choose your chores, and there are plenty of them." She handed me the list and went back to peeling potatoes. The list only had a few things listed, but there wasn't anything that I could do that would only take a couple of minutes. I read the list repeatedly as if something would change from when I first read it.

"Just how many of these things do I have to do?" I asked.

"How many do you think you should have to do?" she asked instead of answering. She looked at me from the side of her eye. "How about we take it one at a time and see what we accomplish," she suggested.

I looked at the list more carefully. I wanted to choose chores that I could finish quickly. For example, washing dishes is easy, but it takes forever; you must dry them and put them away. My mom has been cooking all morning, and there are lots of dishes to be washed. No way! Washing dishes is out of the question. Cleaning the patio chairs and tables is easy, and I could finish it fast since there are only a few. I can spray them with soap and hose them down. I did not need to dry them because the heat from the sun would take care of that.

"I'm going to clean the patio table and chairs. I can knock that out in a minute!" I hurried out to the backyard.

"And take your time, so you clean them well!" Mom yelled. "And be careful around the grill!"

"OK," I yelled as I raced down the stairs. The chairs were stacked in a corner like they were in time out. I hurried to set up the tables and chairs. Then, I went to the side of the house where we kept the hose and a bucket. I was cleaning chairs and tables like a madman. It took a lot less time than I thought it would. Once I cleaned the table and chairs, I felt a great sense of accomplishment. One chore down and the closer I am to getting to play my video games. I backed up to look proudly at my work, and before I knew it, I backed into the grill. I felt the most excruciating pain in my back. I tried not to scream, but I couldn't help it. I let out one big yell, and before I knew it, my mom and dad flew to my rescue.

My mom saw me standing by the grill, and she knew what had happened. She lifted my shirt and grabbed ice from a nearby cooler. I stood still as I let her take care of me. My dad gripped my shoulder and helped me keep still.

"You had one job." my dad said as he snickered.

"James!" Mom retorted. "This isn't funny."

"Too soon?" Dad asked, feeling guilty for joking around. "I'm sorry little dude. I thought I could make you laugh."

"It hurts, Mom," I said as I looked at her with sad puppy eyes. Although it hurt, it wasn't that bad. I was milking it for attention at this point.

As my mother grabbed a bottle of cold water from the ice cooler to wet a paper towel, she couldn't help but notice all the clean tables and chairs set up perfectly for the family get-together.

"Wow!" Mom said. "Somebody was out here working hard."

"Very nice!" my dad said as he looked around the yard. "Did you do this?" he asked.

"Maybe you should take it easy for a little bit," Mom said as she gave me a gentle hug. "You've had a pretty busy morning," he said.

With that, I was excused from doing the other chores. My back was sore, and I wasn't in the mood to play video games. But I didn't want to sit around and wait for my cousins to come either. My mom and dad escorted me into the house, where my mom put ointment on my injury. I felt ninety-nine percent better, but I was still in a weird mood.

My dad came into the room with the tackle box and fishing rods. He is meticulous, and I knew he was about to clean all the items and put them back in place. My accident with the grill must have made me have an out-of-body experience because I shocked myself with what I said next.

"Can I help?" I asked. My dad looked at me as if he were checking to see if it was me.

"Of course, you can help. How does your back feel?" he asked as he placed the tackle box on the table. "You're not just setting me up to get in trouble with your mom or something, are you?" he laughed. "I already apologized for the joke."

"Nah, you're good. I just want to help." I answered. *Where did that come from?*

"What about your back?" he asked as he raised my shirt, checking out the burn.

"It hurts when I move around, but I'm okay," I answered. "Did you see how mom ran out of the house when she heard me yell?" I asked, laughing.

"I was closer to the door than she was when we heard you," he said as he put my shirt down. "She almost knocked me over trying to get to you. I didn't know what was going on," he chuckled. "I think she skipped a few stairs as fast as she got to you."

As we joked about Mom's heroic actions, I laughed so hard my back was starting to hurt. My dad must have seen the expression on my face that I made from the reaction to the pain.

"All jokes aside, Jamal," he said. "We want

you to be safe at all times. There will be times like this when you get hurt, but just know, we will be there to make you feel better and see you through the hard times," he said as he handed me wipes to start cleaning the hooks and bobbers.

"What about when things are rough in our neighborhood?" I asked.

"When times get rough, we are still with you," Dad said with a confident smile. "We are here for you and will protect you. You should be fearless like me. When you look for things to go wrong, they usually do."

My dad and I only talked a little while we cleaned and organized the tackle box. I had a lot to think about, and my dad allowed me to process what he had just said. Then, he put the box away and went back to doing other chores on the list my mom had created for us.

I stood in the kitchen window and watched my mom arrange food on the table, and my dad put food on the grill. I could not help thinking about how fast they came to my aid when I needed them,

and I felt good knowing that they were here for me.
I know things could have been a lot worse. I
thought about how my mother warned me to be
careful of the grill when I went to clean the tables
and chairs. I was determined to get the tables and
chairs cleaned so I could get back to playing my
games. I was not careful at all. Even though I made
a mistake, my mom and dad were there. They did
not have to say I told you so because I had already
suffered enough. I did not want to think about the
scar I would have from the burn or how people
would react when I went to the pool when they saw
it. My mom always says that scars are like tattoos
but with better stories, but I don't think this scar
will have that great a story.

Chapter10

Make it Make Scents

Cousins and friends that had just seen one another last month at my uncle's fish fry were greeting each other like they hadn't seen each other in years. One by one, they marched into our backyard. Some were empty-handed, and some had platters and bowls of food. My mom greeted everyone while my dad was at the grill.

As my mom welcomed one of her co-workers, she called me over to her. The woman gave me a look that suggested she would squeeze my face tight. However, it was too late to pretend I didn't hear my mom calling me, so I slowly made my way to them.

"Jamal, this is Ann from the office," she said, reaching for my hand. "Do you remember her from our last get-together?" she asked.

"Yes. I think so." I answered as I tried to break away quickly.

"Ann wants to give you something," she said as she pushed me over to Ann.

Oh no, I knew it. Here comes a big squeeze.

"Look how handsome you are!" Ann squealed. "Last time I saw you, you wore a shirt with racing cars." She said as she leaned in and pinched my face. "I take it you like fast cars. Am I right?" she asked, reaching into her purse.

"Yes! I do! I do like fast cars!" I declared with a big smile as I looked to see what she was reaching for.

My mom pulled me back when I nearly had my head in Ann's purse.

"Here ya go!" she exclaimed.

She pulled out a shiny, old-school, red Camaro. It was hot! I thanked her for the gift, and she pulled me close enough to give me a giant squeeze. I usually find being squeezed by someone you barely know creepy and annoying, but I had no objections this time.

I went to the side of the house where I could roll the

car on the sidewalk and wait for my cousins. At first, I wanted to use the car to display with the other hot cars in my collection, but I was bored waiting on my cousins. Shouldn't they be here by now? Where are they? I walked to the front of the house to look for them. My uncle's car was nowhere in sight, and there were plenty of parking spaces on the street. I decided to stay in front of the house and wait on the porch.

I sat on the bottom step while looking at my new car. At the sound of every car coming down the street, I stopped to see if it was my uncle. After constantly looking for my uncle, I grew tired of waiting. I stood up and moved the car slowly along the bricks of my house. I became engrossed with playing with the car and no longer paid attention to anything else.

"Hi, Jamal." a small soft voice said from behind me. I turned around and saw it was Dymond. She was walking her miniature pinscher. He looked as though I was interrupting their stroll.

"Oh. Hi, Dymond." I responded, trying not

to seem excited to see her.

"Smells good," she said, looking toward the backyard.

"You too." I stammered, trying to put the words back into my mouth.

"Huh?" she inquired with a look of confusion.

"What I mean is, you do too? You know, like I was asking, that's all. It was a question. I wasn't saying you smell good because you don't. I don't know what you smell like because I can't smell you. I just meant I, too, think the food smells good. So, if I do and you do too, you think it smells good too." I said, desperately trying to fix the words I was carelessly spitting out of my mouth.

Dymond laughed as she and her dog walked away. "Ok, Jamal. Whatever that means." She said, looking over her shoulder. "I'll see you tomorrow."

I sat on the porch, replaying what had just happened. What was I thinking? Did I just tell Dymond that she did not smell good? There was no way to recover from that. She will think I'm rude and will never speak to me again.

I tried not to think about what had just happened, so I sat and rolled the car across my lap. I started looking for my uncle's car again to get my mind off Dymond. My cousins are usually here early so they can eat all the food and hog all the games. Where are they? I jumped from the stairs and headed quickly to the backyard. Halfway to the backyard, my mom was coming to look for me.

"There you are," she said. "Let me take a look at that back." She turned me around and examined where the grill had burned me. I knew Dymond was probably still walking her dog, and I did not want her to see my mother babying me.

"Mom, I'm fine," I exclaimed, trying to pull my shirt back down.

"Well, excuse me for trying to help." my mom retorted. "What's gotten into you?" she asked with concern.

"Nothing. I'm fine," I answered. "Thank you. But I really am fine." I said, looking to see if Dymond was looking. "I'm just tired of waiting for

Tony. Where is he?" I asked, hoping to change the subject. My back was still sore, but I did not need the attention my mom was giving me.

My mom raised my shirt again to look at my injury. She was more concerned with my well-being than whether or not people were looking. Dymond was nowhere in sight, so I allowed my mom to examine my back.

"Your uncle will be here soon with your cousins," she answered as she carefully pulled my shirt back down. "Looks like you should take it easy when your cousins get here?" she suggested. "I don't want you wrestling while recovering from the burn. I mean it!" she insisted. "Make sure Tony knows he can't tussle with you," she said as she gave me that 'I'm watching you look.'

"Yes, ma'am. I know to be extra careful." I answered. The whole time I was plotting how I could take Tony down before he could get to me.

There were no children at the fish fry, and I was bored. Our neighbor Angie had a tiny baby, and people were hovering over her to see the baby. I was not impressed. If you've seen one baby, you've seen them all. I wanted kids my age at the barbeque, and there were none. I paced around the food table and the card table making several trips to the front yard to see if I saw my cousins pulling up. Every car I heard going past our house had me stretching my neck to see if it was theirs.

My dad and his friends sat down to play a game of cards, and one invited me to the table.

"Hey, little man, come watch me as I beat your dad in a game of Blackjack. Come and learn a little something," he said as he pulled out a chair next to him.

I hoped watching them play would keep my mind from waiting for my cousins. I did not have anything to lose since everybody at the get-together was having a good time except me. Grown-ups surrounded me. They talked, but I was not interested in anything they had to say. It was all boring grown-up talk, so I joined my dad and his friends at the card table.

I tried to keep up with the card game but

was distracted. I kept looking for my uncle and my cousins. I watched the men throw down one card after the other. The game moved fast, but I was able to keep up. Finally, my dad's phone rang, and he looked over at me after checking the caller ID.

"What's up, man?" he answered. Then, after a long pause, his eyes met mine, and he quickly turned away and lowered his voice. "Now that's too bad," he whispered. "No. No. We understand. They shouldn't come here around the rest of us. No need to get everybody else sick." he said as he checked to see if I was listening. "Alright then. We'll see everybody next time. Give everyone my best." he said as he hung the phone up.

"Was that Uncle?" I desperately asked. "Are they close?" I inquired, nearly jumping out of my chair to head to the front yard again.

"Your cousins woke up with mild colds, so they aren't going to be able to join us today," he said as he looked for a response from me.

"They should be okay if they come here!" I suggested. "We can stay in the family room and play games away from everybody. I won't let them get me sick," I insisted.

"Well, we don't want to take any chances," he chuckled, and so did his friends at the table. "Besides," he continued, "I can't let them bring the cooties around our friends and family. So, I'm not going to do anything to risk the health and safety of anyone." he declared. "There will be plenty of other times for you to see your cousins," he reassured me as he put his winning cards on the table. "Blackjack!" he said as his friends moaned in defeat.

This is so annoying. First, I burned myself like a klutz, then I made a fool of myself in front of Dymond, and now I don't have anyone to play with because my cousins are sick. This day has been full of surprises, and I don't like surprises.

Chapter 11

Know Your History

My mom and her friends were setting up to play a game of Black History trivia. My dad got her the game last year during Black History Month and another set of questions the following Christmas.

"Can I play?" I asked my mom and her friends. My mom looked at her guests, and before she could ask them, her best friend, Malika, had already answered for everyone.

"We don't take pity on youngsters, so you better bring it if you're gonna join us in this game!" Malika said.

It was each man or woman for themself. Some of the questions were easy. Other questions about the year the event took place were not.

For example, one of the questions was about the year of Rev. Martin Luther King, Jr. Day was established as a national holiday. Everyone looked at me, but I did not have a clue. I remember talking about the special day, but we only briefly discussed when the holiday was made official.

"1980," I blurted out. I was wrong. King's birthday was established as a national holiday in 1983. I know his birthday is on January 18th, and we celebrate the holiday on the third Monday of each month. Why couldn't that be the question?

Even though my answer was wrong, Malika suggested I get points for being so close to the actual year. Malika was the one that said she wouldn't pity youngsters, but she gave me hints throughout the game. Like when it took me too long to figure out what Daniel Hale Williams was famous for, Malika cupped her hands over her heart and made them look like a broken heart. Then, she put her thumbs together and slowly closed the top of her curved hands to make them look like she had repaired the heart. At first, watching her do this was awkward because I thought she was telling me I broke her heart. Then it hit me: Dr. Daniel Hale Williams was the first to perform open-heart surgery successfully. After that, I was on a roll with Malika's help.

"What Black inventor was considered the Black Edison?" my mom asked as she read the card she pulled from the pile.

"Oh, I know this one!" Malika slammed the buzzer and yelled, "Give me a minute!" she stalled.

"I'm sorry, Malika, but you don't have a minute." my mom explained. "We gotta keep this game moving. If you don't know the answer, someone else will have to answer." Mom said as she pointed at Ann. Of course, I wanted Ann to get the answer since she gave me a cool car, but my loyalty was to Malika. Malika had been looking out for me for the whole game.

I stared at Malika to get her attention. She softly pounded her fist into her hand's palm while thinking. Then, as she looked around the table at the players, I finally got her attention. Then, making sure she was the only one looking at me, I moved my lips without making a sound.

I mouthed, "Gar. Ret. Mor. Gan."

"Oh, I give up!" Malika sobbed.

"It's Garrett Morrison!" Ann answered.

"Sorry, Ann, the correct answer is Garret Morgan," my mom said as she placed the card in a pile and pulled another.

"Let's not cheat. Okay?" Malika leaned over to me and whispered.

"I wasn't cheating. I was just giving you the answer." I answered.

"Yeah, sweetie. That's what we call cheating." she quietly laughed.

"Why did you give me the answers to my questions?" I asked her, demanding clarification.

"I didn't give you any answers," she whispered. "I may have given you credit for only missing an answer by a little bit. And maybe I gave you a hint here and there. But I never gave you any answers," she explained.

Mom and Dad always say that angels are always watching over me and are with me to protect and guide me. Malika is like an angel here on Earth because she always watches me. She always helps me see things clearly and reinforces things that my mom and dad have told me. Malika is also my godmother. She vowed to take care of me if anything ever happened to my parents.

"Are you two ready or are you gonna sit there talking to each other?" my mom asked sarcastically. She takes trivia and other games very seriously.

We all got back into the game and answered a few more questions. Malika eventually answered the most questions correctly, making her the winner. Ann came in second place, and I was third. I shuffled the cards and put them back in the box with the buzzer. After using the cards two or three times, my mom pulls out the easy ones and only keeps the challenging ones until my dad gets her another set. After congratulating Malika, people left the game table and headed to the food.

I did not have an appetite. I pushed the chairs under the table and stretched my neck to look at the gate as though my cousins would suddenly appear.

"I'm sorry your cousins couldn't make it today," Mom said as she raised the back of my shirt to check on my injury. "I know you were looking forward to seeing them."

I was embarrassed that she raised my shirt to check on me, but I was glad she was watching my back.

"It's fine," I said, hoping my mom wouldn't feel bad for me.

"No. It's not fine, but I'm glad you are taking it well," Mom said. "I would probably go crazy if I were a kid stuck with a bunch of boring grown-ups." she laughed.

"It's not so bad." I continued, "you guys are pretty cool."

"We are?" Mom asked as she looked at me with uncertainty. "I wonder if you will still think we are cool when you are a teenager." she snickered. "You can go play your video games if you like. I won't keep track of how long you're on them, just don't stay on them too long."

Chapter 12

Mission Unaccomplished

I had been on my video games for what felt like hours. I was hungry, but I could not think about eating. I was doing well in the game, and the next level was calling me. I was in the zone. Then, I heard my dad come into the house and go into the kitchen. He was moving things around and making noise. I could tell he was pretty busy, but so was I. Usually, I spring to see what he is doing, but I can't right now. I am so close to the next level; nothing can stop me. Well, almost nothing.

"Hey, man," he said, taking more stuff from the refrigerator. "How are you doing in here?" he asked.

I couldn't answer him; I was on a mission. Now was not a good time for me to be distracted. I had to stay focused.

"Hey!" he snapped. "Come up for air," he demanded.

"I'm fine," I answered as I continued to play the game.

"How's your back feeling?" he asked as he slowly walked into the room.

"It's good. I'm fine." I quickly answered. I could feel him getting closer and closer. But I did not stop playing my game because I was getting closer and closer to the next level.

"You are really into this game, aren't you?"

he asked as he sat beside me.

"Um-hum," I muttered, not wanting to stop playing the game to respond. At that very moment, I had reached the point where I would get to the next level when my dad put a bowl of slaw down and raised my shirt to look at my back. Instead of hearing bells and chimes of victory indicating I had made it to the next level, I heard doom sounds. Instead of a banner waving congratulations, a flag waved in bold letters, GAME OVER. I worked harder than I had ever worked before to get to the next level. Now I will have to start all over again.

"You heal pretty fast," he said. "The swelling is gone, and there is no redness," he said as he put my shirt back down.

"Dad!" I exclaimed. "I told you I was fine! My back is ok. You and Mom can stop checking on it." I said, trying to check my tone.

"I know you must be upset about your cousins not being here, and perhaps you were more into your game than I thought," he said, "but you better watch your tone. This is not like you," he said in a stern voice.

"I'm sorry." I whimpered, hoping he would take pity on me. "I wish my cousins were here, but today has just been full of bad breaks."

"Bad breaks?" he picked up the bowl and gestured for me to follow him into the kitchen.

I hoped he would get back to entertaining his guests, but it did not matter. Dad wanted to talk, and I had to listen.

"What kind of bad breaks have you been having?" Dad asked.

"You know, just stuff," I replied.

"No, I don't know, and I won't know unless you tell me," Dad said as he waited patiently.

I wanted to get back to my games, so I had to give him an abridged version of my day. I tried to decide what to say and what not to say. Although I wasn't sure what to say, I wouldn't dare mention how I made a fool of myself in front of Dymond.

"Well, I guess I just miss my cousins," I said, getting ready to head back to the video game.

"I figured that was it," he said as he pulled

me back to face him, "No matter what, our health is a priority. You can see your cousins anytime." He said as he picked up the bowl and headed to the door.

I should have left it at that, but no, I had to open my big mouth some more.

"I know. I just wish my cousins were here so I could have someone to play with," I said, still trying to make a break for it.

"Just because they can't come over doesn't mean you can't have fun with them," he said as he grabbed Mom's laptop. "I can put you on a video chat so you guys can talk." He opened the computer and logged on.

"No! No, thank you," I yelled. I didn't want to video chat. Instead, I wanted to play video games. "I'm good, Dad. As you said, I can see them another time." I hurried and dashed to the sofa. Then, jumping on my favorite spot in front of the television, I grabbed the remote and started a new game.

"Okay," my dad said in an unsure voice.

"Let me know if you need me."

"Yep. Will do," I said, glancing over my shoulder, watching to ensure he was leaving. I twisted my body to look over my shoulder, and my back hurt like nobody's business. I had to endure the pain until I was sure my dad was out of the house. I wanted to scream, but he was close enough to hear me. I held it in as I repositioned myself. Pain or not, I'm reaching the next level. I do not want any more interruptions. My parents want to look out for me, but I'm not a baby. Besides, I never get to play video games long enough to reach high levels. They never let me get on social media to check out the latest dance challenges.

I played video games for a few minutes more, never reaching a new level. Finally, it started to get old, and I was bored and frustrated. I shut the game off and headed toward the back door. As I passed the kitchen table, I remembered that my dad had logged into his account.

I grabbed my mom's computer and searched social

media for the latest dance challenges. I spent the next few minutes laughing at crazy videos and doing extraordinary dances. Then, after trying a breakdance move I saw an influencer doing, I landed hard on my back. It hurt more than when I got the burn in the first place. I had no business being on social media platforms without supervision.

Something told me not to get on social media, and now I guess it was my angels trying to warn me not to disobey my parents. I was in a lot of pain, but I held my breath so I wouldn't scream. I knew my parents would come in and check on me soon. I could feel the tears racing down my face, but not as much as I could feel the sting of pain on my back. I had to think of something quick. I shut down my mom's computer and went to look in the mirror to see if I was bleeding. It was hard to see my back, and I must have looked like a dog chasing his tail as I looked over my shoulder from one side to another, trying to look at my injury. I thought my shirt would be drenched with blood, judging by how bad the pain was.

My mother walked into the house with empty dishes and put them on the counter near the sink. I had to be careful of my facial expressions. She knows me well and can pick up on the slightest hint of disorder. I don't know how she does it, but she always knows when something is wrong.

"Did you get enough to eat?" she asked as she washed her hands. "And how about your back? Do you think I need to look at it?" she asked as she dried her hands.

I didn't know what to say. I wanted my mom to take me to the ER, considering how much pain I was in, but she would see that I was on her computer and doing dance challenges on social media if she got any closer. I had to say something quick because silence is a bigger whistleblower than a facial expression.

"I'm fine, but I can still show you my back." I answered quickly, heading over to where she was.

"Is something wrong?" she inquired. "Why do I get the feeling you're not fine?"

"No. I am fine. My back hurts a little bit, though." I said as I looked back to see if she could see that I had moved her laptop.

"Let's see what's going on with this burn," she said as she turned me around and raised my shirt. "Well, your dad was right," she said, pulling my shirt down. "He said that when he checked on you last, there was no redness or anything, but if it hurts, I can put some ointment on it." she offered.

What is she talking about? What does she mean that there is no redness? It feels like I should have blood all over my back. There must be swelling or something. I took a nasty fall with my breakdancing moves.

"No, thank you. I'll pass on the ointment." I hesitated as I thought about it.

"Alrighty then. Let me know if you change your mind," she said as she kissed my forehead and headed to the back door.

"I will be fine. I'll come out in a few to grab something to eat." I said as I watched her open the door to leave. I was glad she did not notice I moved her computer. If she did, I would have had to explain why I was on social media, and she would have figured out that I was doing a dance challenge and hurt my back. It was a narrow escape, but an escape nonetheless.

"Oh, and Jamal," she said as she peeked back in, "stay off of my computer."

Chapter 13

Sunday, Sunday, Sunday

For the first time in a long time, I went to sleep without hearing police sirens or gunshots. As rough as things usually are out there, last night was peaceful. Maybe the sounds were there, and I was in a food coma from overeating at the fish fry. I awakened to the smell of bacon. I was surprised to awaken hungry after eating so much the day before, but the smell grabbed me and escorted me to the kitchen.

Nevertheless, I was ready for a good Sunday breakfast with my mom and dad. My dad doesn't eat bacon or other pork. He likes it, but his dad had health issues, and my dad believes my granddad died from poor eating habits. It's rare, but every once in a while, Dad will grab a piece of bacon or an occasional pork chop. My mom doesn't allow me to have too much pork, but there is always bacon on Sundays.

"Good morning," I said to my mom while she was flipping pancakes.

"Well, good morning." my mom said, looking over her shoulder. "How's your back feeling this morning?" she asked.

My back? I completely forgot about my back. I must have been in a deep sleep because I do not remember feeling any soreness. I slept like a baby, or at least how my mom says I slept when I was a baby. My mom always boasts of how well she had it because I always slept peacefully through the night as a baby.

"It feels a little sore when I think about it, but not that much," I answered. "Can I wake dad?" I asked.

"No. Let your dad sleep. You guys had a very busy Saturday. We'll get him up in time for church."

She said that as if she didn't have a busy day. There were tons of dishes in the sink before I went to bed. Now the kitchen looks as though the fish fry never happened. My mom and dad always wash and put dishes away together after hosting fish fries and other events. I help them every once in a while, but not last night. I usually hear them laughing and talking about how much fun they had while they cleaned the kitchen together, but not last night. I don't even remember when or how I got to bed.

"Go ahead and wash your hands so you can eat and get ready for church." mom cheerfully said.

I washed my hands and sat at the table. It takes me only a short time to finish my meals. I knocked out three pancakes and two strips of bacon like they were nothing. My mom, on the other hand, was eating slowly. I was already chewing my second or third portion when she finally took one small bite of her food.

"Are you able to taste the food when you eat that fast?" she asked.

Even though I laughed, I did not slow down. I wanted to finish eating so that I could wake my dad. We usually do something special together as a family on Sundays. I walked over to get the milk from the refrigerator, and before I could bring it to the table, I heard sirens. I knew it wouldn't stay peaceful for long.

"Mom!" I snapped. "Let's move away from here!" I said as I pushed my plate away. I no longer had an appetite. I covered my ears as the sirens got closer and louder.

"Move for what?" she said as she pushed my plate closer to me. "Your dad and I love it here, and we thought you did too." She continued eating as though the discussion was over.

"It is too much crime here," I said, resting my head on the palm of my hand.

"There's too much crime everywhere." she said, "we can't just pick up and move every time things get bad. What about your friends? Your school? That girl you like?" she laughed.

"They should move too," I answered confidently. "Wait, wait, wait!" I said, just realizing that she said I liked a girl. "No way! I do not like Dymond at all," I remarked.

"Oh, is that her name? Dymond?" my mom asked sarcastically. "I wasn't sure, but now I know."

"Know what?" I stuttered. "There is nothing to know. She just goes to my school. We are in the same class, and her locker is across from mine. She has a cool dog and likes to jump rope. I've seen her in the neighborhood, but that's all. That doesn't mean that I like her." I blurted out. I may as well have told my mom that her favorite color is blue.

"Oh, I see." Mom laughed. "You have no interest in this girl." She said as she looked at me over her glass of milk, taking a sip.

"No. I don't like her. I just want to move." I snapped. "I hate it here!" I yelled. I was upset about the sirens, but I also was embarrassed that my mom thought I liked Dymond.

"Calm down," my mom said firmly. "Hate is a pretty strong word, Jamal. I hope you know what it means to hate since you're throwing it around so freely." She got up, grabbed my plate and hers, and took them to the sink. "Some people around here have it bad and do what they think they have to do to put food on their plates and survive, but they don't necessarily hate us," she said as she started washing dishes. "I believe they like it here too, but they wish their lives could be a lot different," she said.

I walked to the sink with her and dried the dishes as we talked. "I never said they hated us. I just know I hate it here. The troublemakers might not hate us, but they sure don't like us." I said sadly.

"If they liked us, they wouldn't make it so hard to enjoy living here," I complained.

"Oh, Jamal," my mom stopped washing dishes and turned around to talk to me. "It's just that they don't know a better way to do things, so they do what they think is best for them, and unfortunately, they turn to crime as a last resort."

"So why can't we move somewhere without crime?" I probed.

"There is no such place," she answered with a smirk. "I don't care where you go in the world; crime will be there if people are there. People are not perfect. We all make mistakes, and we usually hurt ourselves and others when we do," she said as she tapped me on the nose. "This is why we have to look out for each other. Your dad and I are here for you, and we will protect you. I've lived here most of my life. I had five brothers and two dogs. I was the youngest and only girl in our house. I had to fend for myself all the time. Or at least when my brothers weren't there to put bullies in check. These streets don't scare me. After all, my mother and father didn't name me Azania for nothing." she said, flexing her arms to make a muscle and then pointing to her brain. "I've had to stand up to bullies and outsmart the best and worst of them without using violence. I never let things distract me from my life goals, and I keep crime and negative things beneath me," she declared. "Your dad and I love you, and we need you to trust us to protect you at all times," she said with a reassuring smile.

"I feel helpless here," I said, sounding defeated.

"You shouldn't," Mom said as she cleaned the table.

"But I do. That's just a fact," I said. "You and Dad aren't always with me. Not at school, not when I go to the park, nor when I am at practice. Then what? How can I feel safe?" I asked.

"That's an excellent question and has a super easy answer," Mom said, stopping and bending down to look me in the eyes. "You don't have to worry about bullies and crime," she said confidently. "All you have to do is believe you can defeat anything that tries to frighten you. Even animals can sense fear in people. Be brave and confident. Most of all, always let us know when something or someone bothers you." Mom said as she continued cleaning up.

Chapter 14

Closet Conundrums

I love waking my dad up on Sundays. I usually run and jump on the bed to startle him, but after talking to my mom about the crime in this rough neighborhood, I wasn't in a playful mood.

"Is it alright for me to come in?" I asked,

knocking on the door.

"My man, Jamal!" He said with a big smile, covering his head under the covers.

I entered the room, although he never told me I could. He was in a playful mood, and I didn't want to put a damper on the moment, so I ran and jumped on the bed as usual. I tried to pull the cover off his head, but he was strong, and I didn't stand a chance. I went to the foot of the bed and crawled under the covers, still trying to get the covers off him. It was useless. His strength also came with speed, and he was always a step ahead of me.

"Dad!" I yelled, "come on, get up."

"Make me," he said as he gripped the covers tighter to ensure I couldn't pull them off him.

There was no way I could get those covers off and make him get up, and he knew it. I thought about telling Mom that he would make us late for church, but I came up with a better idea.

"Ouch!" I yelled in agony. "My back," I said with an exaggerated moan.

Immediately, my dad threw the covers back

and got up to check on me.

"Hey, you alright," he asked. "I'm sorry about that. I forgot all about your back."

As soon as he reached for me, I started pointing and laughing. "I gotcha!" I said victoriously. I never outsmart my dad. He usually catches on to my pranks. I could tell he was surprised that he fell for it. He smacked himself on the head and gave a big chuckle.

"You little phony," he said as he shook his head and helped me off the bed.

"And the award for best actor goes to me, Jamal!" I said proudly as he began making the bed. Dad walked to his closet and stared at the clothes in front of him. He pulled the clothes back and forth on the rack but did not choose anything to wear. Instead, he looked over his shoulder at me and then back at his clothes.

"Why don't you pick something nice for your old man to wear to church while I go and jump in the shower?" he asked.

"Me?" I asked, surprised.

"No. Your cousin, Tony." he laughed as he gestured for me to come to the closet. "Of course, I mean you!" he said.

"Well, okay, but what do you want to wear?" I asked without thinking. He wouldn't have asked me to pick out something if he already knew what he wanted to wear.

"Surprise me." He said as he headed out of the room.

I walked over to the closet and looked at his clothes. He did not have many clothes, and most looked the same. In the corner of his closet, he had his uniforms hanging together. He works as a manager of an oil change place. Before he was a manager, all his shirts had oil stains. They would only come out after mom washed them several times. My mom would fuss when he put them near her things even though she knew they were clean.

I pushed past all his uniforms, T-shirts, and sports jerseys. He had dress shirts, but only a few. It did not take long for me to get to where his clothes ended, and my mother's clothes started. She had all kinds of blouses, dresses, skirts, and pants. Her things were packed in the closet, making it hard for me to move anything on the rack. As I pushed her stuff off my dad's clothes, I saw a tiny T-shirt that looked like it could fit me. But I knew it wasn't mine, and there was no way it would fit my mom or dad.

My curiosity got the best of me. I could barely reach the shirt to see it completely, so I tugged at it to see it better. In my struggle, I broke the hanger it was on. The shirt fell in my arms. There was an airbrushed picture of a young boy smiling, with the words, R.I.P. Xavier.

I stood holding the shirt and staring at the picture. I knew it was my dad's friend Xavier. It was eerie because Xavier was my age when he died. He even looked like me, only his hair was shorter. I stared long and hard at Xavier's picture on the shirt. Then, I started thinking about what my dad and I had discussed at the park. My dad must still miss his friend, having kept the shirt for so long. Xavier was so young. If only he and my dad didn't argue.

Perhaps he would still be here. My dad must feel responsible for his death. Maybe he is keeping the shirt out of guilt.   These thoughts ran through my mind with many others. I did not realize how long I stood staring at the shirt. I snapped out of my stare when I heard my dad come out of the bathroom. I did not have anything picked out for him to wear. There was no way I could hang the shirt back up, so I balled it up and threw it in the closet. I quickly grabbed a red polo shirt and khaki pants and ran to sit on his bed.

I could see the T-shirt on the closet floor from the corner of my eye.

"Here ya go, dad," I said as I pointed out his outfit. "I'll grab some shoes for you too."

My dad looked displeased at the clothes on the bed. He didn't notice that I started heading to his closet. I hoped to grab the shirt and bury it behind my mother's shoeboxes.

"No. No. Don't worry about shoes. I'm wearing the ones in the hallway," he said as he walked over to the closet and closed it. "I guess I'll be going to church looking like I work at a country club or selling car insurance." he laughed.

I couldn't stop staring at the closet door. Once someone opens that door, they will see the shirt on the floor. There wasn't anything I could do. Even if I could get into the closet, it wouldn't do any good. I broke the hanger, and I didn't see another one. Anyway, I can barely reach the bar to hang the shirt back on it.

I could hear my dad's music playing from the bathroom, so I knew he would be heading back there. I wanted to tell my dad what happened, but he was in such a good mood I did not want to spoil it.

"Are you alright?" he asked while I stared at the closet door.

"Yes. I'm fine." I assured him, thinking he would return to the bathroom where his music was playing. I waited for him to leave the room for a chance to retrieve the shirt.

"Great!" he said as he escorted me to the door. "Do me a favor and turn the speaker off in the bathroom."

The door closed behind me as I went down the hall to turn off the speaker. I could see my mother sitting in the kitchen, watching the news on her laptop. I walked into the kitchen and joined her at the table.

"Can I ask you something?" I asked as I sat down next to her.

"Of course!" she answered.

"You know Dad doesn't like talking about what happened to Xavier, right?" I asked, catching my mom off guard. "Is it because he feels guilty?" I asked.

"I think it makes your dad sad when he thinks about it, but talking about it is therapeutic for him. He and Xavier were like brothers. You didn't see one without the other." she said as she shut her laptop and continued, "Xavier has been gone for a long time now, and your dad has made many friends since then. He will never forget all the good times he had with him, nor will he forget the tragedy. But he chooses to keep the good memories closest to his heart. Life will always have ups and downs. Your dad decided long ago that he would not let the downs of life bring him down with them. It is not his fault Xavier was shot, so he has nothing to feel guilty of," she said as she reached for my hands and pulled me close. "Your dad told me he talked to you about Xavier at the park yesterday. Do you still have questions about him?"

"No. No more questions," I answered. "I wondered why dad had that shirt with Xavier's picture in his closet," I said.

"That old shirt is still in the closet?" she said, thinking aloud. "I thought it was in a storage box under our bed." she laughed. "The shirt is a keepsake and a reminder never to let petty things ruin great friendships. Xavier's death was a wake-up call to many of the boys in the neighborhood. He did not die in vain. Many kids stopped getting into mischief after Xavier was killed." she said as she stood up and pushed in her chair. "Wait. How do you know about that shirt?" she asked me surprisedly.

"I was picking out an outfit for dad to wear,

and it fell. I tried to hang it back up, but the hanger broke, and I couldn't find another hanger, nor could I reach the bar to hang it on," I said desperately.

"Well, I don't want you to worry about what happened to Xavier. I know it may be hard to understand right now," she explained. "But life goes on." she said as she headed to their bedroom.

I did not want my mom to tell Dad about me blundering in the closet. I could tell he was not very pleased with the outfit I picked out for him, and now he will know why it took so long for me to pick such a simple outfit. I also did not want her to tell him we talked more about Xavier. I could hear her open the closet door. Hopefully, she will just hang the shirt back where it fell.

Chapter 15

Moments and Memories

Our church was close enough to walk to, but we took the car when we had somewhere to go after service. Dad likes driving, but after dealing with cars and customers at the shop all week, he wants a break from cars. He also doesn't like paying high gas prices to fill his tank.

Today, we jumped in the car and headed to church. That means we are going somewhere after church, or we have to pick up one of the neighbors and bring them to church.

"Where are we going after church?" I asked, looking at my parents, wondering who would answer first. "Do we have to pick up Mrs. Johnson today?" I asked. My mom looked at me and smiled but did not answer my question. "I'm glad we aren't walking today," I said, hoping one of them would respond, but they didn't.

The ride to church was quick and quiet. We did not pick anyone up to bring them to church, so that could only mean one thing; we are going somewhere after church. But where? Or maybe they don't want me to walk because I hurt my back yesterday. I wished one of them would have just answered my question. Now I'm going to think about this during service.

The service seemed to drag, and I kept looking at the clock. I desperately wanted to know where we were going when service was over. I felt myself nodding off throughout the service, and my dad gave me a nudge each time. It would perk me up for a little bit, but I still had side effects from the food coma from the day before.

"Sit up straight, and don't fall asleep." my dad whispered. I tried to stay awake and alert for the rest of the service. But, when I looked at the clock, it looked like the time had not changed. I wanted desperately to know why we drove to church. Where on earth could we be going when service is over? I could not stop wondering.

When the children's choir stood up to sing, I saw Dymond. She was standing in the back row. The pianist struck the keys with one loud stroke, and the choir began to sing. I honestly did not hear anyone but Dymond. She was the only choir member that I saw. Everyone else was a blur. I no longer listened to the piano or anything. I only saw and heard Dymond singing in an angelic voice.

My dad nudged me again, "Didn't I say don't go to sleep." he whispered. "You slept all night and then some. How is it you are still sleepy?" he asked as he straightened me up. Little did he know I was not asleep. I was in awe as I watched Dymond sing.

Finally, service ended, and we stood and prepared to leave. As we walked down the aisle heading to the door, my mom spotted Malika. They started to chat with one another as we walked out of the church. Whenever those two get together, we end up staying at the church for a while. They spoke as my dad walked to the car. I hung around with my mother to remind her that we had somewhere to go. I didn't know where, but I was eager to find out. Malika was excited to tell my mom about her new dress, and my mom had to show Malika her new shoes. Why couldn't they talk about this stuff last night? They just saw each other at the fish fry.

I saw my dad waiting by the car and giving some of the fellas a high five or a fist pump as they passed him. Then, he pulled out his phone and started dialing. Shortly afterward, my mom's phone began to vibrate. I knew it was my dad, and so did she. She didn't look at her phone; instead, she hugged Malika and grabbed my hand. Then, we walked quickly over to the car.

"You knew that was me calling, didn't you?" Dad laughed.

"Of course," she laughed. "I'm glad you called because we would still be talking if you didn't." Mom laughed.

We got in the car, and I looked at them both. I waited for someone to tell me where we were going. "Are you guys going to tell me where we are going?" I asked.

"Nah!" they laughed as they answered in sync.

I rested my chin on my fist and stared out the window.

"Just kidding, Jamal." Dad laughed. "It's no secret or surprise," he said, glancing at me in the rearview mirror. "We will take a quick trip to the cemetery," he said. I was hoping this was just another one of his jokes. "I usually go every year on Xavier's birthday, but since you're curious about him, I thought I would bring you along." my dad glanced in the rearview mirror at me again.

"Jamal, I told your dad what happened with the t-shirt today, and he was fine with it. It was no big deal, but he would have rather you told him about it than me." She looked back at me with a big, beautiful smile.

"We don't hide things in this family. Feel free to ask us about anything or talk about anything," my dad said.

"You're not in trouble or anything like that, but it is always best to be open and honest. We are here for you." my mom confirmed.

"That's right," Dad said. "It's like what Pastor talked about today in church," he said, looking in the rearview mirror at me again. "I know you were dozing off, but do you remember what he said?" he asked.

I did not remember anything the pastor said. I couldn't stay focused when all I could think about was where we were going after church. I do, however, remember that beautiful song that

Dymond was singing.

"Pastor told us how important it is to talk to God and ask Him for help because He is always with us and will always help us. It's the same with us. We're your parents, and we are here for you, and you should always feel comfortable talking to us about anything.

The drive was long and peaceful. The farther we got away from my neighborhood, the more peaceful things were. Finally, we drove by a beautiful golf course, and I sat up to look at the golfers as they walked across the beautiful green grass. Next to the golf course was a cemetery. I had never been to a cemetery and didn't know how I felt about going there.

I looked at the cemetery and then back at the golf course. I wondered what it must be like to relax and play golf without worrying about crime or hearing gunshots and sirens all the time. As we passed the golf course, I imagined being one of the golfers strolling on the green and only having to think about my target and taking my swing.

"Here we are," my dad said as he parked. He sounded like we had just arrived at an amusement park instead of a cemetery. "We'll leave the car here and walk to Xavier's plot. Watch where you step; there are a lot of grass markers everywhere." My dad pointed to a headstone that was flat in the grass.

Plots. Grass markers. You don't hear those words often, but I knew what they were. I stepped over them carefully as I tried to read out the inscriptions on each one. I had only ever seen cemeteries in movies while watching something scary. I thought I would feel uncomfortable, but strangely, I didn't. This cemetery was very different from what I saw in movies. This place was peaceful. Perhaps, it was because I had my mom and dad with me every step of the way. We walked a little farther and saw headstones that ranged from small to extremely tall.

My dad stopped as we reached a headstone with tiny hands closed together in prayer carved on the top. Right below the hands was Xavier's full name. At the bottom of the headstone was the date of his birth, followed by the date of his death. I sneaked a peek at my dad and watched him look at the monument. To my surprise, he did not look sad. Instead, he stood there with a smile.

"Here you go," he said as he turned his eyes to me, "Here lies Xavier, my childhood best friend, and brother." He did not seem bothered at all that he was standing over the body of his friend, whom he would never see again.

"Are you okay, dad?" I asked him as I walked closer to him.

"Yep," he answered cheerfully. "I'm more than okay. Xavier was a good kid. I know that for sure. He was a good kid that got mixed up with the wrong kids. I feel good knowing that he is in a much better place." he said confidently. "I miss him, but I have very fond memories of him, and that will never change," he said as he walked closer to where my mother was standing on the other side of the headstone. I walked closer to the gravestone, staring at the tiny hands.

"Can I touch it?" I asked my dad.

"Of course, it's just a headstone. Nothing will jump out at you," Dad said with a big smile and a chuckle.

I reached out to touch the top of the headstone, and as soon as I came in contact with it, something grabbed me by the shoulders.

"Rah!!!" my dad yelled and gave me a tight tug. He and my mother were laughing hysterically as I nearly peed my pants.

"That's not funny, Dad," I yelled as my heart raced a mile a minute.

"I'm sorry, Jamal, but I could not resist." He continued to laugh as my mother came to hug me.

"He was just kidding around, don't be mad at him," she said as she held me close. "Are you okay?" Mom asked.

"I'm fine!" I growled as I walked away. "Can we go now?"

I went back over to Xavier's headstone. Again, I reached out to touch it, but I watched my dad ensure he didn't get any bright ideas this time.

Then, finally, my dad approached me as I ran my fingers across the letters in his name.

"I'm sorry, Jamal. I only wanted to startle you, not make you angry," my dad said as he reached his fist out for me to pound it.

"Why do you come here on his birthday? Is today his birthday?" I asked.

"No, today is not his birthday." He answered. "I'm not big on visiting gravesites, but I use this visit to remind me to appreciate life and to remember all the fun Xavier and I had together as kids. We did many fun things in our neighborhood, and I feel you are missing out on that fun because you are afraid to go outside," he said.

"But things were different when you were a kid," I said.

"Things weren't that different. Our neighborhood still had a great deal of crime. There were many fights and gang activity back then," he said. "Although guns were not as easily accessible as they are now," he continued. "Knowing what happened to Xavier when he was young reminds me that I must cherish every moment of life, not just for me, but for my family. You are all important to me and I will always be here for you." my dad got a little emotional as he continued, "You can depend on me whenever you need me. When times get rough...."

"I know, Dad," I said as I reached for his hand, "you are always with me," I said, finishing his sentence.

"That's right, and I always will be," Dad said, gripping my hand.

Chapter 16

Beauty in the Rough

It was unseasonably warm, yet there was a cool subtle breeze. As we returned to the car, I looked at the cemetery. There were headstones as far as my eyes could see, no matter where I looked. My dad was pointing out where famous people were buried. He named people buried in the cemetery that were related to us. It was hard for me to concentrate on what he was showing me. There were grass markers of every size everywhere we stepped.

As we walked, I wondered about each person buried at the cemetery. I wondered how they met their demise, how old they were, whether their families missed them, and whether they missed being alive. I did not want to think about ever being buried here, but it crossed my mind. Just thinking about it for a moment put me in an uncomfortable mood.

"I'm hungry!" dad blurted out, "what does everyone have a taste for?"

I, for one, did not have a taste for anything. Therefore, I could not think about food while walking to the car through the cemetery.

"After yesterday's indulging," mom said, "I think we'll stick to something light." Mom suggested as she threw out the name of her favorite restaurant. She turned to look at me, hoping I would agree with her choice, but I didn't say anything.

Finally, we made it to the car. Once we were all in and buckled up, dad started the car. I tried to stop looking at the gravesites, but I couldn't help it.

"Humm," Dad mumbled, "it's so convenient that the place where we can grab something light just happens to be your favorite restaurant," he laughed. "But I'm down with that if Jamal is good with it too," he said as he looked back at me.

"I'm not hungry," I responded as I looked at all the headstones. How could they think about food in a place like this?

"Well, that's too bad because I'm not

spending a dime on popcorn and candy when we get to the theater. That stuff is way too high," Dad said firmly. "I think you better build up your appetite and help us decide where we will eat," he said as he drove out of the cemetery.

"Fine," I said in a low grumpy voice. "Mom's spot is fine." It took me a minute, but when I finally processed what my dad had said about the theater, I sat up straight and looked at my mom, "Wait, what?" I asked in excitement.

They both laughed, and we were on our way. As the headstones slowly faded away as we got farther away from them, the green of the golf course became more visible. There was more green grass on the golf course than in our entire neighborhood. I stretched my neck to look deeper into the green. I could see fountains and small ponds. Everything was beautiful and peaceful.

I knew it wouldn't be long before we were back in reality. There would be no beautiful fairways or fountains, and we could kiss the serenity goodbye. I knew it would not be long before we saw graffiti-marked buildings and people hanging out everywhere.

"Why can't we move here?" I asked, interrupting the conversation my mom and dad were having. "Don't you guys want to live somewhere quiet, like here?

"I love the peace we have in our community," my mom answered, "it may not always be quiet like here, but I enjoy the peace I have living where I feel welcomed," she asked.

"But it is so much better here than where we live," I answered, thinking that was enough to convince them.

"Wow," mom said as she turned around to look at my dad. "Let me see," she continued. "We just left a cemetery and passed a golf course, and we weren't there an hour, but you've concluded that it is better than where we live?"

"Jamal," dad joined in, "we were the only people at the cemetery. If we heard people making noises, we wouldn't have hung around to see who was making the noise. Cemeteries are quiet for obvious reasons," he said. "I don't think comparing the cemetery with where we live is fair." He said, shaking his head.

"I always hear sirens, helicopters, and people yelling at each other where we live. We should look for somewhere quiet to live." I said, still hoping to convince them that we should move.

"You mean to tell me," Mom said as she turned to me, "you never hear the sounds of birds chirping and children laughing where we live?" she asked. "Those are the things I mostly hear when we are at home. But I guess we hear what we want to hear. Or…," she paused, "what we focus on hearing. Your dad is right; it is not fair to compare a place with very little life with a place full of life." she said confidently. "We live close to the police station and a firehouse, so we should expect to hear noisy sirens. Also, the golf course has to be quiet so the golfers can concentrate on their next move without distractions. So, of course, we will not hear noises from there.

"Exactly!" I confirmed, thinking she opened

a window of opportunity for me to make my point. "I need to concentrate and focus on my homework, and it is nearly impossible with all the noise in our neighborhood." I blurted out with confidence. Now, they will have to consider my request.

"Jamal, you're a good student. I believe you do pretty well under the circumstances." my dad reminded me. "You have what's called resilience," he said as he looked at my mom, and they nodded at each other as though they scored a point.

It was useless. My parents were not interested in moving, and there was nothing I could say to make them reconsider. I decided not to challenge my dad on his comment about being resilient. Instead, I leaned closer to the window and watched the scenery change. After passing the golf course, I started seeing gas stations and some nice stores. When we passed the freeway, it was all downhill from there. Things began looking rough as usual, and I knew we were back in my hood. The stores in our neighborhood looked less pleasant than the ones by the golf course. The closed stores were boarded up and decorated by local graffiti artists.

Mom believes I see and hear these things because this is where I focus, but I don't just wake up and say something like, I wonder how many gunshots I'll hear today or how many sirens will disrupt me. I look forward to peaceful days, but they are few and far apart.

"Did you hear that siren just now?" my mom turned to ask me.

"What siren?" I inquired as I looked out the window. That's when I heard the siren in the distance. My mom didn't have to say a word. I knew she was trying to prove her point. I admit I didn't hear the sirens until she said something, and that's when I thought about it.

"I hope you get used to being in this neighborhood for a while," mom said. "We aren't going anywhere, but you can best believe you will have the best of everything we have to offer you while we are here."

"That's right," dad interjected. "No matter how rough you think things are, we will be here for you and see that you are safe," he said. "You shouldn't live in fear, Jamal. You've got to let that fear go and enjoy life while you can," he continued. "We are almost at the restaurant, so think about what you want to eat. We can pick a movie once our bellies are full."

My dad switched the subject seamlessly. I know my dad was speaking the truth because I always feel safe with them around. And honestly, even when they are not around, I still feel a sense of security. When I get hurt, they always make me feel better. So as much as I didn't want to admit it, I knew I had to start looking at the bright side of things.

We drove in silence as Dad's music played quietly in the car. My mom's eyes were closed, but I could hear her softly humming along to the music. I continued to look out the window at the neighborhood. I could see my school in the distance. The old building looked depressing, but I had a lot of fun at school. I have many crazy, cool friends I would miss if we moved.

As we drove deeper into our neighborhood, I saw kids playing ball in the vacant lot across from the school. I chuckled as I heard them laughing. Cars passed us with their music booming, and noisy buses went back and forth. Greedy birds were squawking as they foraged for food. I could hear everything but sirens; thankfully, I did not hear any gunshots. The more I focused on the sounds that made our neighborhood come alive, the more I did not hear unfavorable sounds.

I started to realize the sounds of the city were alright. I even had more appreciation for the sounds. If sirens were blaring, I did not notice them. It was a beautiful day, and it could only improve as we spent the day together.

As we passed our local meat market, Mr. Mario gave us a friendly wave as he swept trash from in front of his store. My dad blew the horn and waved back at him. Next to his butcher shop is a liquor store that is usually pretty busy on Saturday nights. The liquor store customers hang out there and leave a mess behind when they leave. Their mess makes a lot of work for Mr. Mario, who does his best to keep things nice and orderly for his customers. Mr. Mario is the best. We get all of our meat from his shop. Once when I was at the meat market with my mom, he told me to catch some fish for him to sell. He also talked to me about carving meat and why it is important to eat right. He warned me about the liquor store and encouraged me to stay out of trouble. He's not afraid of anyone. People don't hang out in front of his store. When people hang out in front of the liquor store, they usually speak to him and share a good laugh. They have great respect for him, and he has the same for them.

I sat straight up as we passed the mobile phone store because I knew we would approach our church soon. Things aren't so rough around the church. The building is enormous, and there are flowers all around it. I never noticed how green the grass is or how grand the stained-glass windows are. There were still lots of cars in the parking lot. The meetings and choir rehearsals ended, and people were coming out of the church.

We slowly passed the church parking lot, and my parents waved at their friends. Dymond and her family sing in choirs at our church, and I was hoping they would still be there. I looked for Dymond but did not see her or any other children. I sank into my chair and leaned my head on the window. When we turned the corner, I could hear children laughing, and there she was. Some kids were playing tag, but Dymond was jumping rope. She stopped jumping when she saw our car, and our eyes met.

I wanted to tell my dad to slow down, but I said nothing. Instead, I sat up straight and smiled at Dymond. I hoped my parents did not see me smiling at her. They would have playfully teased me all the way to the restaurant, the theater, and the ride back home. To my surprise, I discreetly waved at her, and she waved back shyly. I could feel my heart racing in my chest, and I couldn't hear or see anything but Dymond. I sank into my chair and closed my eyes.

My mother was right about focusing on the

beautiful things in life. Our neighborhood is full of beautiful things and amazing people. They've always been here; my parents have known this all their lives. The park and the pond were here during their childhood; I should enjoy them and make lasting memories as they did.

The best thing about my neighborhood is that it has my family and friends. No matter how rough things are, they are here for me, and I will have to give our neighborhood a chance. Even with all its imperfections, our neighborhood is not as rough as I thought. I can't do anything about crime and chaos, but I can have peace knowing that life is good and there is a Dymond in the rough.